REVIEWS FOR DEATH OF A ZEN MASTER

Cornelia Feye's Death of a Zen Master is a well-written and absorbing story that harkens back to the classic murder mystery novels such as those penned by Agatha Christie. I loved the isolated setting for the crime and relished seeing the fear and suspicion of the students as they realize they are trapped with a killer, with no way out and no way to contact the outside world. Feye's characters are finely crafted and true-to-life and her plot is ingenious. She gives the armchair sleuth plenty of red herrings to consider along with Greg Stern, as he tries to unmask the killer and stay alive. This classy, modern-day homage to the golden age of murder mysteries is most highly recommended.

5 star review by Jack Magnus for Readers' Favorite

Attention to spiritual detail juxtaposes nicely with the elements of a murder mystery investigation as Greg - the main protagonist - is forced to evolve on several different levels to handle adversities which feel both familiar and alien at the same time.

It's intriguing to see his personal evolution in the course of the story, even when a near-confrontation in a forest evolves into an appreciation for nature and quiet: *"The sun warms my back. I smell the pine scent of the forest around me. Freedom. Take this, Abbess Clarita. Freedom is not always in the mind—it is in putting one foot in front of the other on a trail in nature."*

Zen ideas and experiences run side by side with Greg's murder investigation and intrigue, creating a satisfyingly revealing story that operates on more than one level. It will especially intrigue readers with any degree of prior interest in Zen Buddhist perception, who will find the premise of a murder and a peaceful monastery's disruption to be thoroughly engrossing reading.

Death of a Zen Master is highly recommended reading for murder mystery fans looking for more spiritual and psychological evolution in their main protagonist than is usually proffered in the typical 'whodunnit'.

D. Donovan, Senior Reviewer, Midwest Book Review

In Death of a Zen Master, Cornelia Feye turns a two week penance at a Zen retreat for a cheating husband into a rollicking whodunnit with more dead bodies than Buddha statues!

Matt Coyle, author of the award-winning Rick Cahill crime series

From the very beginning of this mystery, set at a Zen Retreat House in the Ventana Wilderness area, the characters are full of life and opinions. Greg is here to pacify his wife and has no intention of embracing anything other than the excellent food. He's willing to go through the motions until Vega forgives him, and that's all. When the Abbess is found murdered and a 300-year-old buddha goes missing, Greg finds something to fill his time and, he hopes, a way to impress his wife. Everyone is under suspicion, and. Everyone seems to have a motive. Feye, who is known for her art mysteries, takes the reader on a clever and twisting route to a satisfying conclusion. The characters are well written, believable and bright. The setting is perfect. Woven throughout the story is just enough Zen philosophy, history, and art history to create a fully evolved novel.

Tamara Merrill, Author of Shadows in our Bones, The Augustus Family Trilogy, and many short stories

Forget your English Manors. And manners. A Buddhist monastery in California makes the perfect setting for this engaging and clever take on the we're-trapped-in-place-and-one-of-us-is-a-killer story. In Cornelia Feye's capable hands, the search for spiritual enlightenment goes hand in hand with the search for a murderer. A tasty Karma-snack of a mystery novel.

Corey Lynn Fayman, author of the award-winning Rolly Waters Mystery Series

A rousing and entertaining mystery in a very unique setting— a Zen monastery. The talented Cornelia Feye has created two unforgettable characters, Greg and Vega Stern. Separately and together they must solve a murder while they immerse themselves in Zen Buddhism. It will keep you guessing all the way to the last page.

Carl Vonderau, author of Murderabilia

DEATH OF A ZEN MASTER

Cordia Feye

DEATH OF A ZEN MASTER

CORNELIA FEYE

KONSTELLATION
PRESS

Published by Konstellation Press

San Diego, California

www.konstellationpress.com

Editor: Lisa Wolff

Cover design: Scarlet Willette

ISBN: 978-1-7346421-3-1

For the strong and fearless men, who are not afraid of kindness and compassion.

PART I

MODERN SHANGRI-LA

1

Day 2: 5:30 A.M.

As far as I'm concerned, a remote Zen retreat has few advantages, but if there is one, it's the utter silence and darkness at night. No streetlights, headlights, car noises, TV sounds, vibrating smart phones; no music, nor any analog or electronic sounds. The reason for this beautiful silence, which enables me to sleep like a rock for the first time in years, is the absence of electric outlets—think: no way to charge your devices—absence of internet and cell phone connections, and very limited electricity, generated by a few solar panels. That's the idea: unplug, disconnect, relax, sleep, and meditate.

But what's the purpose of this precious predawn silence if exactly at 5:30 every morning a runner tears through the quiet community vigorously shaking two huge bells, making a gigantic racket? I can't stand it, but it's part of the penance my wife, Vega, imposed on me.

Right in front of my small redwood cabin with the shoji window screens, I see the runner's flickering headlamp and curse those damned bells shattering my deep sleep. Moaning,

I bury my head deeper into the pillow on my futon; but then the runner comes back for a second round on his return through the cluster of huts. I consider rolling off my futon onto the tatami mats, when I remember that the 5:30 bell is only one of several calls to morning meditation. I have at least fifteen more minutes to lie here in the dark.

I force myself to review the elaborate etiquette required before entering the Zen-do meditation hall. A lot of rules precede sitting in meditation to do exactly—nothing. Yesterday at my orientation a young, aspiring Buddhist nun explained them to me. The rules include a lot of bowing, but then again not to everybody, only at the right times and places. When entering the Zen-do—first with the foot closer to the doorframe—I have to bow to the Buddha statue, and then approach the Ino. Don't bow to him. He is just a kind of usher giving out seat assignments, meaning I will be instructed to sit at the spot of a regular monastic who isn't there. Whisper, whisper, the third spot from the corner on the right. Load up with pillows and black cushions, because my knees don't bend so well, especially if I have to sit there for an hour before daybreak.

Reaching my empty seat, I have to bow to it and to the white wall behind it. Yes, that's correct, I have to bow to a wall; don't ask me why. I didn't dare ask my pigtailed instructor for fear of a highly abstract, long-winded explanation. I'll just do it. It's all part of my penance.

Then I have to put my pillows down on the raised platform, sit down, and swivel around to face the wall without touching the wood with my feet. This is very important, I was told, because during serious practice periods the monastics spend the whole day in the Zen-do and eat off this part of the platform.

I shudder thinking about spending a whole day in meditation. One hour is torture enough. Yesterday my legs fell asleep, my shoulders were screaming with pain, and my back was killing me, not to mention my mind was in an uproar, wanting to get up, get a cup of coffee, go back to bed.

My pigtailed almost-nun (as a real nun she's going have to shave her head) told me stories of the olden days, when a Zen master—or maybe it was just the Ino—walked around behind students' backs and hit them with a stick when they slumped over in exhaustion.

Did I remember everything? Here is the next reminder to get up. Not a bell this time, but a wooden peg banging onto a wooden tablet. The banging gets louder and faster with urgency. Only five minutes left.

I roll off the futon and slide into my black sweatpants and long-sleeved T-shirt. Modesty and dark colors. Wouldn't do to show up at the Zen-do in bright red or neon green. No need to wash or comb my hair. Nobody's going to see me anyway. They'll all be facing the wall with their eyes closed. Even if I wanted to spruce up my appearance, there's no mirror. Now the wooden sticks are banging at a frantic speed.

I step into the cool air outside and slip into my flip-flops deposited in front of the door. I look up at the brilliant, still star-studded sky through the dark branches of an oak tree. The air smells of moist earth and dry leaves. I join other dark and quiet figures on the main path making their way to the meditation hall. As we cross the wooden bridge, I hear the low bubbling of the creek below.

Another perplexing rule of pre-meditation etiquette: once I sit on my pile of cushions hopefully settled down for the duration, the Zen Master walks by behind, inspecting the backs of his charges. I am supposed to sense his presence or hear his bare feet on the wooden floor and bow at just the moment when he passes my seat. That bow is meant to move like a wave through the rows of students. Surely a beautiful sight, except no one besides the Master can see it.

I've reached the Zen-do and quietly take off my shoes to store them in the shelves provided. I make my way to the front door, modestly covering one hand with the other in front of my belly. The students are stepping, bowing, entering. Most are shorter and either much younger or older than I. I suppose most men my age have neither the time nor the inclination to go on lengthy Zen retreats midweek. They are at work. Where I should be.

But I can do this. I promised Vega. This is my atonement for having a tiny affair—totally insignificant really. Just a one-night encounter at a conference. It wasn't even good and I regretted it immediately. I love Vega and don't want to lose her, and her condition for taking me back is this two-week stay at the monastery. To confront my feelings, become aware of my thoughts, and learn how to interact sensitively with women. One day down. Thirteen more to go. I can do this. I step, bow, and shuffle into the dimly lit meditation hall.

Something is wrong. Students are gasping, scattering, moaning in the middle of the Zen-do. You are never supposed to be in the center of the hall, only around the sides. Even I know that. What happened to all the etiquette? I'm completely confused, but apparently so is everybody else.

6:00 A.M.

In the center of the hall on a raised platform reserved for the abbot of the monastery sits a voluptuous, middle-aged African American woman dressed in monastic robes. She is completely motionless.

She shouldn't be sitting there. Meditation hasn't started yet. Students are still taking their seats, doing all their elaborate prep work. But nobody is doing that either. They are just milling around in total confusion. I'm getting curious and politely push through the throng of people surrounding the platform.

Holy Christ—sorry, I mean dear Lord Buddha—what happened here? An ugly red line runs around the neck of the woman and an orange rope lies curled on her lap. Her hands are folded and her eyes are slightly bulging. Otherwise she sits peacefully in perfect meditation pose. I can't tell if she is ghostly pale, because, well, you know, her skin is dark. But I've seen plenty of corpses and I know this woman is dead. I feel the rush of adrenaline that always accompanies a crisis. This is the kind of stuff I have to deal with in my normal life. I just didn't expect it here.

"Okay," I say to the frightened pigtailed nun-in-training next to me. "She's dead. Where is the Zen Master? The abbot?"

"She *is* the Zen Master. She is—was—our abbess," she hisses back.

Oh shit. I had no idea. When I bowed to the presence passing by behind my meditation seat, I imagined a tall, slim, white man with a stick. Go figure. Goes to tell you that we all have our prejudices, as Vega would say.

Somebody has to take charge of the situation. Now that the Zen mistress is dead, it's not clear who it's going to be.

There is only one outside phone line in the monastery office— for emergencies. Clearly this qualifies. Someone has to call the police. The usually calm, composed, and poised Zen community is fluttering around the meditation hall like moths surrounding a flame. They are curious, scared, and horrified all at the same time.

I raise my voice, even though that is completely against etiquette. Lord Buddha will forgive me. "Did someone call the police?"

Everybody stops mid-movement and looks at me.

"I'll go and do it," says Brother Jacob, whom I met yesterday when he was manning the office/gift shop. Yes, there is a gift shop selling crystals, T-shirts, and Buddhist literature.

Now that's decided, everybody settles down. A senior monk in flowing black robes speaks up.

"It will take several hours before the police get here, so let's all do what we are here for. Let's meditate for the peaceful transition of Abbess Clarita."

Chastised, monks, nuns, and students shuffle to their seats. I didn't even get my seat assignment and cushions yet. I thought I was going to get out of meditation today. No such luck. The Ino irritably points me toward Brother Jacob's empty seat. I sigh and scramble over to the platform loaded up with pillows.

The room settles down. The senior monk passes behind me and I bow. Finally nobody fidgets anymore, nobody coughs or shifts. We all breathe in and out as one. I hear a bird call outside. The sun must be coming up by now. I admit, it's nice when this happens, the quieting, the stillness, the comfort of being here with a room full of people devoted to peace. The joint sigh of relief of settling into the present moment.

The peaceful feeling doesn't last long—not for me. My knees start to hurt. How can I sit here and meditate quietly with a dead body right in our midst? It doesn't seem to faze the others. They must know something I don't. At least no one touched the body. The police will be grateful.

7:30 A.M.

A little bell announces the end of the meditation session. Finally. I couldn't have done another minute. Of course I can't just jump up and run outside, as much as I want to. We all have to exit in an orderly, ritual fashion, bowing and all.

Outside I find myself next to the pigtailed Zen apprentice. She smiles at me. I smile back.

"Nomi," she says and extends her hand.

"Greg," I say and shake it.

"Thanks for getting everybody's attention in there."

"No problem. I'm very sorry about your abbess."

"It's terrible. I can't understand it. Who would want to harm her? She was practically a saint."

We grab our slippers and move along.

Nomi is kind of cute, I think, as I watch her walk toward the dining room. Dark and petite, with a sweet smile and dimples. I catch myself right away. I am not supposed to check out cute girls here. That's what got me into trouble in the first place. But I didn't mean it that way. Plus, she's going to be a nun, and she's not my type anyway. I like tall, blond women like Vega. But this one, she's sweet.

7:45 A.M.

We walk across the central path to the dining hall. It's not open yet, so the monastics and guests mill around in the open space equipped with a few benches and tables overlooking the creek. I go to the outdoor counter that provides tea and coffee and pour myself a cuppa joe. Thankfully coffee is allowed here, even though it is a mood-altering beverage. Must be because it wakes you up, and Zen is all about waking up—after all, the name Buddha means "The Awakened One." Gratefully, I sip my mug of coffee with almond milk and watch the scene unfold.

About twenty members of the monastery, including volunteers and ten guests, stand around uncomfortably. Not all of them made it to the morning meditation, but they all look like they would love to get out of here.

Easier thought than done. Only one treacherous dirt road leads over the mountain pass to the retreat center. Most guests use the stage or shuttle option, where they leave their cars at the end of the paved road and then get a ride with a four-wheel-drive monastery transport vehicle from there. They're stuck. We all paid for the privilege of cutting all electronic and physical connections to the outside world. Now, we wish we had some modern communication and transportation devices at our disposal.

One of the guests, an Indian-looking man in his late thirties with thick, curly black hair and a twitch in his left eye behind the wire rim glasses, walks over to me. He has smooth cream-colored skin.

"You're one of the guests, right?" he says.

"Yeah, my name is Greg Stern."

"I'm Rakesh Paneer. How long are you here for?"

"Two weeks."

"Oh man, that's a long time. I was scheduled to get out of here tomorrow, but now I don't know."

"You may have to hang in a while longer."

"I'm afraid, once the police get here, there will be interviews and such," he agrees.

"The murderer has to be one of us. I can't imagine anybody getting in or out, especially not at night. We would have heard an engine if someone had arrived, and the road is barely passable even during the day."

"You're right. I hadn't thought of that," Rakesh admits. "I came here on the stage. My car wouldn't have made it. Did you drive?"

"Yeah, I have four-wheel drive. But it was scary, especially the downhill after the crest. The ruts are so deep. I think I ruined my brake pads slowing down the car. And that was during daylight."

Rakesh nods. "I can only imagine that road at night."

"Is there any other way the killer could have come in here? Maybe by creek with a canoe?"

Rakesh shakes his head. "The creek is so shallow you can cross it just jumping from rock to rock. A little farther down by the narrows small waterfalls tumble over the rocks. No boat could navigate that."

"What about hiking in?"

"It's over twenty-five miles of treacherous terrain. It

would take at least a whole day to hike in, or out. The murderer would meet the police on their way in. Plus the gate is closed at night."

We stand for a minute, sip our coffee and listen to the people around us, who are talking with great agitation. One word jumps out of the conversations: *why?*

"Why would anybody want to kill the abbess?" Rakesh asks, echoing the talk around us.

"I have no idea, but I have a feeling the police are going to ask the same question."

Rakesh's eyes widen in distress. I'm fascinated by his thick, black eyelashes. His twitch becomes more pronounced. "I can't stay here any longer. I have to get back to work."

"You may not have a choice. Where do you work?"

"In Silicon Valley, at LinkedIn. I came here to get away from the constant stress and pressure for a few days."

He still sounds pretty stressed to me. "So you live pretty close?"

"Just a few hours, but a whole world apart. Why are you here?"

"My wife insisted I come here to reflect and, well, reform, I guess."

"You do something bad?"

"Something like that."

He nods. "What do you do for work?"

"I own a private security firm."

"No shit! You sent mercenaries to war zones, like the Blackwater outfit?"

It's my term turn to smile. People usually immediately make the connection with Blackwater when they hear what I do. But it's actually much more harmless. "No, we mainly supply companies with security guards, sometimes we provide bodyguards for celebrities or politicians."

"So you must have a military background?"

"Law enforcement. But that didn't go so well. I do better being my own boss."

"I hear you. Making your own rules sound good to me," he says with a lopsided smile.

"Lots of rules here." I let my eyes sweep the scene in the courtyard.

"True, but it's also blissfully remote and the food's really good." Rakesh looks at the dining room door longingly.

"It's delicious. I gotta get their cookbook. I love the fresh-baked bread, and how about that blackberry tart in phyllo dough yesterday? I wouldn't mind some meat once in a while, though. Are you vegetarian?"

"I grew up Hindu; I have never eaten meat in my life. So I don't miss it."

"Good for you. I wish the dining hall would open soon," I say, as my stomach grumbles.

8:30 A.M.

Uneasy restlessness ripples through the crowd, as a senior monk in flowing black robes strides down the trail from the monastery gate escorting four police officers. A pathway opens to the middle of the courtyard as people step aside to let them through. The senior monk raises his hand and everybody is silent.

"Dear members of the *sangha*," he begins.

I'm pretty proud of myself for knowing that *sangha* is the term for a Buddhist community.

"For those of you who don't know me, I'm Osho Haku, and I'm the acting abbot in the absence of Abbess Clarita. We have all been through a terrible shock and suffered a great loss, but we have to stay calm." He speaks with authority and without any emotion. "The police got here as fast as the road allowed, and we must cooperate with them in every way. These officers from the Carmel Valley PD are going to take statements from each of you. So, stay within the monastery compound; don't hike down to the Narrows or on any forest trails. You may go to the hot springs, the dining hall, or your cabins."

"Thank you, Osho Haku," a red-faced, bulky officer, whose nametag reads José Rodriguez, calls out. "We're examining the crime scene. The monastery will provide us with a list of your names. We'll come and find you to get your statements, or you can come to the monastery office, where two officers will be posted. In the meantime, don't leave the monastery."

I make a mental note to ask Nomi who Osho Haku is.

At that moment, the double doors of the dining hall open and we gratefully stream inside.

Murder always makes me hungry.

9:30 A.M.

Despite the lack of bacon or ham, the breakfast of warm, home-baked rolls, fresh fruit, nuts, and more coffee is more than satisfying. After my belly is full, curiosity gets the better of me.

Brother Jacob, Osho Haku, and Nomi are in the Zen-do examining the crime scene with the police. I climb the stairs to the Japanese-style meditation hall, stash my flip-flops, and tiptoe quietly on bare feet around the wooden veranda surrounding the hall. Through the open windows, set high in the walls, I can hear but not see what's going on inside.

"Did the abbess have any enemies?" I identify the baritone voice of Officer Rodriguez.

"No, sir. She's been the head of this community for two years now, and she was well liked," says Osho Haku.

"She was beloved," interjects Nomi's weepy voice. "We can't imagine why anybody would want to harm her."

"Is anything missing?" asks Rodriguez.

A moment of silence. Apparently they are all looking around.

"Oh my Lord," Brother Jacob exclaims. "How could we not have noticed?" He sounds pretty upset.

"What's missing?" Rodriguez prompts.

"The Buddha statue," Haku says in a low voice. "This is absolutely devastating," he adds. "It's a gilded wooden statue of the Buddha Amitabha from Japan's Edo period. It stands on a pedestal next to the platform of the abbess."

I can hear Nomi sobbing quietly.

Rodriguez clears his throat. "Was it valuable?"

"Priceless, monetarily and spiritually," Brother Jacob says hoarsely.

Vega will be very upset when she hears about the missing Buddha statue.

"And nobody noticed it until now?" Again the voice of Rodriguez.

"We were all busy processing Abbess Clarita's death, and then we meditated facing the wall, so we didn't notice the Buddha statue was missing," Brother Jacob recalls.

"You sit facing the wall?" Rodriguez asks in exasperation.

"Yes, in *zazen* we face the wall to minimize distractions."

"What's *zazen*?" Rodriguez asks.

"*Zazen* is the type of sitting meditation we practice here," Haku explains.

Rodriguez sighs. "Are you sure the Buddha statue was gone when you first entered the hall at, what, six A.M.? Or could somebody have taken it after you left following your meditation?"

A reasonable question. I try to strain my memory. Did I see the Buddha when I first entered? I can't remember.

"I'm not sure," Haku admits.

So much for the new Zen Master's mindfulness, I think.

"The Amitabha Buddha statue was over three feet tall," Nomi says. "It should be hard to hide and easy to find."

"How heavy was it?" Rodriguez asks.

"I'd estimate about sixty pounds," Jacob says.

"Okay, not easy to carry. We'll search all the buildings and take statements from all the guests. Perhaps someone will remember seeing the Buddha when they first entered the hall. In the meantime, we need a photo of the statue."

I sneak away quietly, thinking that this puts a new spin on the case. Is it possible that an art thief wanted to steal the Buddha and Abbess Clarita got in the way?

11:00 A.M.

Now that art theft is part of the mix, I really must contact Vega. After all, she's the art expert in the family. Plus, I have to tell her what happened. Let her know what she's got me into.

Everybody is eager to contact their loved ones, so there is a line of about twenty people in front of the telephone in the office. Two of the police officers have set up tables and are taking statements. It's hard to hear anything above the din. We're told not to give out any unnecessary information about the incident. Just tell our families that the abbess is dead, that we are all safe (hopefully, I think, since we obviously have a murderer in our midst), and that we'll be detained here for a while longer. When I finally get Vega on the line, she moans. "Oh no, not the Amitabha Buddha! It's from the Edo period It's three hundred years old. A priceless piece. God forbid something happened to him."

I'm a bit annoyed at this reaction. "It seems everybody is more distraught about the Buddha statue than the abbess."

"No, that's absolutely horrible too. She was such a wise, kind teacher, and a wonderful human being with a big heart and a great sense of humor."

"I didn't get to meet her. But you might consider that I'm stuck out here with a killer. We could all be in danger." I want her to feel a little bad for me, or at least show some concern.

"I'm coming out," she declares, but if I had any illusions that it's because she's worried about my safety, she dispels them immediately.

"I know this statue better than anybody. After all, I helped the monastery find it in the first place. I may be able to help. For example, did they take the mandorla as well?"

"I have no idea what you're talking about. And I'm glad to hear you are so concerned about my welfare."

"You'll be fine. The police are there, aren't they?"

"Four officers and more on the way. I have to go; people are waiting to use the telephone. How are you planning to get here? They're not running the stage."

"I'll figure it out. See you soon."

I'm sure you will, I think as I hang up and hand the receiver to the next person, who snatches it impatiently.

It will be nice to have Vega around, but she can be a bit bossy sometimes.

11:30 A.M.

I walk back to my cabin, since I really don't feel like standing in line to give my statement at the office. Along the way I see Nomi working in the monastery garden, a beautiful space with blooming flower beds, benches, and shade trees. She is weeding a bed of pink zinnias. The bright flowers and Nomi create a striking image.

"Hi, Nomi. Want some help?"

She looks up and pushes a strand of hair out of her face, giving me a nice smile showing her dimples and pearly white teeth.

"Thanks, I'm fine. I feel better doing something instead of standing around worrying. Weeding always clears my mind."

"I hear you. I couldn't handle that crowded office any

longer either. Everybody talking at once. If the police want my statement, they'll find me. Did they already talk to you?"

"Yes. They asked me if I saw the Buddha statue when I first entered the Zen-do, and I hate to admit it, I don't remember. So much for being mindful and aware," she laughs ruefully.

I remind myself that I'm not supposed to know about the missing statue, and ask, "Is the statue missing?"

"Yes. Do you remember seeing it when you first came in?"

"No, but somebody out of all the people there must have seen whether it was there or not."

"I suppose so. Osho Haku has called a meeting tonight. Maybe we'll find out more."

"What does Osho mean?" I get a chance to ask.

"Osho is a high-ranking priest. One who has been with the monastery for many years and put in at least ten thousand hours of meditation. He has received *dharma* transmission and is qualified to teach students."

"And what does *dharma* mean?"

"*Dharma* is the teaching of Buddha."

I'm impressed with the 10,000 hours but decide to save the explanation of *dharma* transmission for later. "He's taking over, isn't he?"

Nomi sits back on her heels and puts down her little shovel. "He's next in line as senior monk. He almost became abbot two years ago, but there were some concerns about his conduct."

This is getting interesting. "What concerns?" I ask.

"An incident with a student at another Zen center. Nothing was ever confirmed. But Sister Clarita was so popular and her books are very successful, so she was elected abbess."

"Abbess Clarita wrote books?"

"Yes, and she gave *dharma* talks all over the country. She's —was—pretty famous in Zen circles."

"So Haku and Clarita were rivals?

Nomi looks at me sharply. "What do you mean?"

"Nothing. Just making an observation. He stepped into his leadership role very smoothly." Plus, he looks like I imagined a Zen Master would, I think, but don't say.

"Rivalry is based on ego. It's not part of Zen behavior," Nomi explains.

Okay, I'll take that into consideration, I think. But based on my experience, striving for power is part of basic human behavior, Zen or not. "How did you get here, Nomi?" I say instead.

She takes off her gardening gloves and gets up. We walk over to one of the benches and sit down in the shade.

"I came here two years ago after leaving my third rehab program. I was a raging alcoholic in my old life."

"I'm sorry, I didn't mean to pry."

"It's alright. I found my place. I gave up the outside world, and I finally found my inner purpose. There used to be a gaping hole inside my soul before I came here."

For a moment we just sit and look across the blossoms and listen to the gurgling creek, as I mull over what she just said about the gaping hole inside.

"How do you do it—the meditating?" I finally ask.

"I take three deep breaths and then I just let the thoughts and emotions come and go."

"That simple, huh?"

"If you've tried it, you know it's not simple at all."

I certainly can't deny that.

12:00 noon

A police officer comes to my cabin to take my statement and fingerprints. I have nothing much to contribute. I didn't know the abbess and didn't notice the Buddha. The officer searches my cabin and asks me not to leave the premises. I ask about the time of death, but I don't expect much of an answer.

"I saw an orange rope on her lap," I probe.

"Okay, what about it?" he says with hesitation and takes a step backward. With his body language, he confirms that the rope is important and most likely the murder weapon.

"It looked like a rope commonly used in construction projects."

"Are you a construction worker?" he asks.

"No. Are there any construction projects going on here?" I ask.

"Not according to Osho Haku," the officer says and departs.

A walk to the bathhouse at the hot springs before lunch seems like a good idea. It will be relaxing to soak in the mineral springs by the creek, even though the sulfur makes the water smell like rotten eggs. All this commotion has taken my mind off my resentment about my exile here. It's actually quite exciting.

I think about Nomi, as I walk along the creek to the bathhouse. What would it be like to give up everything— your house, your furniture, your profession, your clothes, your friends—and commit to a place like this? To be at peace. *But is she really at peace?* the old skeptic in me wonders.

The bathhouse is divided into a men's and a women's side. It's clean and newly tiled, with an indoor and outdoor spa, and a large wooden deck overlooking the creek. A few stone steps lead down to the shallow brook for a cool-down dip in the icy water.

I shower and slip into the outdoor spa underneath the oak trees. The branches loom overhead in the receding fog. The fog was dense this morning. It probably helped the killer to conceal and carry off the Buddha statue.

Six men already sit in the steaming outdoor tub discussing the case. They make space for me.

"They say the time of death was between two and five A.M.," one of them says. I recognize Rakesh with his long, black lashes, but nobody else.

"That's not much help," another man says. "We were all asleep."

"It's so quiet here. Wouldn't someone have heard a struggle in the Zen-do?"

"And why was the abbess up so early?"

"Apparently she often went to meditate early when she couldn't sleep."

"What about the Buddha? Did any of you see him when you first came into the Zen-do?"

Shaking heads all around.

"I did," Rakesh says. We all look at him, surprised.

"Are you sure?"

"I have a photographic memory. I told the police the statue was on its pedestal at six A.M. I was very fond of this Buddha. He was always the first thing I saw in the mornings. He looked so balanced, peaceful, and calm. That's how I want to be." I notice that his eye doesn't twitch.

We all sit silently for a minute, slightly embarrassed by this personal revelation.

Finally I say, "Well, that's significant."

1:00 P.M.

At lunch I sit next to a burly man with a red face. We spoon up our curried butternut squash soup and take big bites out of the homemade bread with butter, followed by an arugula salad loaded with pecans and pumpkin seeds.

"I'm Greg," I introduce myself. "I sat next to you in the hot springs a little while ago."

He turns to me and extends a callused hand. "Bill Mason," he says.

"Nice to meet you, Bill. What brings you here?" I'm intrigued, because it's hard to imagine why brawny Bill would want to come to a Zen retreat.

"We're doing some construction down by the yoga center, past the bathhouses," he explains.

"So there is construction going on here after all."

"Yeah, why not?" he says defensively. "There's always work to be done in a place like this."

"It's just that the rope used to strangle Abbess Clarita is common on construction sites and Osho Haku denied any projects were going on right now."

Bill gets very red in the face and a vein in his thick neck is throbbing. "I won't have me or my crew implicated in this murder, just because we're not as holy and spiritual as the rest of this bunch here. We're honest, hardworking men."

"I didn't mean to imply anything. I just pointed out a contradiction," I say reasonably. He calms down a bit.

"Well, maybe I overreacted. I'm just tired of people looking down on me."

"Is that happening? Zen is supposed to be nonjudgmental."

"I don't know anything about that. I just don't fit in here."

"Me neither," I admit.

We eat in silence for a minute. The pumpkin-seed bread is crusty on the outside, soft and chewy on the inside, and still slightly warm from the oven. I gotta get that cookbook.

"At least the food's good and the hot springs are relaxing." I say to break the uncomfortable silence.

"They let us eat here and use the hot springs, because there's nowhere else to go, and there are no showers in the cabins."

"Gotcha. I wasn't questioning you."

Bill nods, apparently appeased. "What do you think happened?"

"It seems like a thief came into the Zen-do in the middle of the night to steal the Buddha, but Abbess Clarita tried to stop him, so he strangled her."

"Seems an awfully big risk to kill the abbess for a Buddha statue."

"Pretty bad karma, if you ask me. I understand the Buddha was very valuable."

He gives me an appraising look. "So, how'd you get here?" he asks.

"My wife made me come."

He grins understandingly.

2:00 P.M.

After lunch I decide to sneak a cigarette before Vega arrives. A roped-off smoking area is pretty far removed from the main compound, beyond the monastery gate, next to the dead-end road, where all the cars are parked. I'm surprised to find pigtailed Nomi there, smoking what looks like a very thick, hand-rolled cigarette.

"Hi, Nomi. I didn't know you smoked."

"I gave up all my other vices, even sex. This is my last outlet." She smiles and blows smoke into my face. I recognize a familiar pungent scent. We watch two kitchen workers and the chef negotiate with a policeman next to one of the monastery vans. They finally come to an agreement and pile into the van, including the policeman.

"They have to make a supply run. With all these people stuck here, plus the police, we need more food," she says.

"Makes sense," I say and take a big breath of her second-hand smoke. "So, about that incident in Osho Haku's past? The one that prevented him from becoming abbot?" I ask, as we sit on the narrow wooden bench, stretch our legs, and stare into the azure-blue sky overhead. It looks as if it goes on forever. Instead of high, it looks incredibly deep.

"I shouldn't talk about it," Nomi says and hands me the joint. "It's not my place."

I take a drag and pass it back. "I know he used to live in another Zen center closer to the city. I'm sure it was much more accessible than this one," I probe.

"Are you kidding?" she giggles. "This is as inaccessible as it gets. You can't get farther away from it all than this."

"Is that why you came here?" I ask.

"Yeah. I used to go to the Zen center in the city. I didn't know anything about Zen until I stumbled into that center, and it changed my life."

"Was Haku there at the time?"

"Yes. I knew him there, just in passing. He never acted inappropriately in my presence."

"But with someone else he did?"

Nomi sighs. "It's so peaceful here. I don't want to think back on those days. There were a lot of troubled kids that came through the doors of that center. I was one of them. This one girl was a drug addict. I remember her. She was really young, strung out. She accused him of touching her inappropriately."

"Did you believe her?"

"I don't know; I wasn't there. Haku did spend time with the girl; he was trying to help her."

"You think the girl made it up?"

"I'm not sure. It's possible. She was in bad shape and not a reliable witness. It was an ugly situation. The girl ended up back on the streets, and Haku's reputation was damaged. That's when they sent him here. Far away from vulnerable people and situations."

"At least you got away from all that, Nomi."

"I'm glad to be here. Far away from temptation—except I

manage to smuggle a few of these joints in once in a while. Want another drag?"

"Absolutely." I inhale and notice the treetops swaying gently like seaweed underwater. The colors of their green branches, speckled by sunlight, are so vivid I almost want to believe that this is an enchanted realm. A deer walks up to our enclosure and looks at us with big astonished eyes. We freeze in mid-motion and stare back. After a few minutes of this standoff, the deer gets bored and disappears into the forest.

"I'm happy you found this hidden Zen retreat, far away from the confusing world out there."

She smiles wisely. "When you stand still, the world comes to you."

I decide this is too deep for me, so I get up and glide back to my cabin for a nice, long nap.

4:30 P.M.

I am rudely awakened from a pleasant dream where I'm floating over the garden and forest of a deer park. Someone shakes my shoulders roughly and urges, "Wake up, Greg, wake up."

I open my eyes tentatively and see Vega's face looking down on me. Her short blond hair looks a bit tousled and her gray eyes stare at me intensely.

"What are you doing here?" I ask, slightly annoyed. After all, she sent me here to relax and unplug. Fat chance of that now.

"I'm waking you up—it's almost evening." She starts to fold and stack my clothes, which are scattered across the floor. Did I mention there is no wardrobe?

"I did get up at five thirty in the morning," I remind her.

"I know, but we are going for a walk." She's all ready to go, in her yoga pants and hooded sweatshirt.

I rub my eyes and ask, "How did you get here, anyway?"

"I hitched a ride with the supply truck. You don't seem very happy to see me."

"You just woke me up. What do you expect? So you hitched a ride with the monastery van?"

"Exactly. I met them at the food store in Carmel Valley, and here I am."

I sit up, because I know from experience that any further resistance is futile. I see her travel bag on the tatami mat of my—now our—redwood cabin. "I can't go for a hike, because the police said we can't leave the compound." There, try to argue with that.

"I can. I wasn't here when the murder happened. I'm not a suspect." Her logic is impeccable.

"But I am," I say defiantly.

"Don't worry, you'll be with me and I can keep an eye on you."

"I don't think it works like that."

She casts me a sly look. "I'm sure you're tired of being cooped up here with nothing to do."

"I was taking a delicious nap when you came."

"Come on, the fresh air will do us good and we'll both get some exercise."

Maybe a little walk wouldn't be so bad. I barely know the layout of this place. "Where do you want to go?"

"Follow me."

That's my Vega; always has a plan.

6:00 P.M.

We march out the door and down the central pathway to the meditation hall, where we take off our sneakers and slip inside.

"I thought we were going for a hike," I whisper, afraid this will turn into another meditation session.

"We are. We're just starting here," Vega whispers back, as she steps up to the pedestal where the Buddha used to sit. She inspects it carefully. "They left the mandorla and there is minor damage to the lotus throne," she mutters. "Let's go out the back way."

We sneak out the back door, put on our shoes, and walk toward the forest and the outward-bound dirt road.

"What's a mandorla?" I ask.

"It's the flaming halo behind the Amitabha Buddha. It's called a mandorla because it's shaped like an almond."

"Aha. You don't really want to take a hike, do you? You don't care about my health and exercise. You just want to find out where the thief could have taken the Buddha," I realize.

She gives me a wicked grin. "Never hurts to combine business and pleasure."

I shrug in resignation. "What's an Amitabha Buddha?" I ask, even though I know it may lead to a lengthy art lecture. But, I might as well know what we are looking for.

"Amitabha is the Buddha of the Western Paradise. There's one for each of the five directions, but he's the most popular one."

Here we go. There's the lecture. Why are there five directions? "East, west, north, and south..." I improvise.

"Plus the center," she adds, completing the list of dimensions. "Amitabha is also known as the Buddha of the Pure Land, a beautiful paradise full of lotus flowers, huge diamonds, blooming trees, and exotic birds."

"No wonder he's so popular," I say, to signal that I'm paying attention. So apparently the ascetic, nonmaterialistic Buddhists appreciate precious stones.

"Most Buddhists believe if they die while praying the mantra of Amitabha, they'll go straight to that magical place."

"That doesn't sound very Zen to me. More like a superstition, or wishful thinking."

She shrugs. "How do you define Zen?"

Good point. I couldn't define Zen if my life depended on it. But being swooped off to a diamond-studded paradise after you die whispering some Buddha's name was certainly not part of my Zen expectation.

"In Japan," she continues, "the entrance gate to the Western Paradise is believed to be at the summit of Mount Fuji."

Oh boy, it gets better and better. Now this paradise even has a physical entrance on a mountaintop. "He was from Japan, this missing Buddha, wasn't he?"

"Yes, from the Edo period, three hundred years old."

"How heavy was he?" I say, trying to steer the conversation to more practical matters, evading another lecture about Edo being the old name for Tokyo.

"Around sixty pounds. Just imagine you had to carry a three-foot-high Buddha, and it was still dark. Where would you go to hide him well, but also have easy access to load him into your car later?"

"Fine, I'll pretend to be an art thief carrying a Buddha." I stagger through the forest for Vega's entertainment, feigning I'm carrying an awkward load.

"The thief left the mandorla behind, which would have made it much heavier and harder to carry. But it also decreases the value of the statue considerably."

Apparently she's not amused. "Let's pretend we are carrying the Buddha between us, assuming there were two thieves. We would stumble over these roots and smash into the tree trunks." I try to demonstrate the impact with the oak trees.

"They could have had headlamps, but the Buddha is so fragile that even carrying him for a short distance would have damaged him severely. Pieces of the wooden throne or a body part would have broken off. The thieves couldn't go far. They didn't have much time, either. It must have been shortly before dawn."

"Actually, it wasn't dark. We established that the Buddha was stolen after meditation. The sun was up." I tell Vega about Rakesh's observation that the Buddha was still on his pedestal at 5:45 when we entered the Zen-do.

"Even riskier. The Buddha can't be far, and he can't be that hard to find." Vega sounds optimistic.

We blunder through the underbrush and scratch our arms and legs on the brambles.

"We're making a heck of a racket," Vega observes. "Someone would have heard the noise, if they were all up at that point."

"Maybe not, because we'd all assembled in front of the dining hall, discussing the case," I remember.

We establish that the Buddha must be hidden somewhere between the Zen-do and the road.

"Let's stop and think," I suggest. *When you stand still, the world comes to you*, Nomi had said.

We pause and listen to the faint rustle of the leaves in the breeze; the tock-tock of a woodpecker; the sound of crackling branches on the forest floor, where small animals scurry about.

"Okay," Vega says. "We need to find a hiding place big enough for the Buddha and accessible from the road. The thief couldn't have buried it; there was not enough time and the dirt would have damaged the statue. No cars, except the monastery van, left since yesterday. So, where could it be?"

"Let's split up," I suggest. "I'll canvass the area to the left of the road, and you take the right side."

Vega nods and disappears between the tree trunks. I slowly scan the forest for crevices, rock caves, indentations, or woodpiles. The light is fading, and I fear we are too late for this search. I sit down on a tree stump for a little break. The forest is cool and shady at this time of day in late summer. The smell of pine trees and moist earth hangs in the air. In this remote valley, inside the Santa Lucia Mountains, we humans are still the rare intruders, instead of invaders who have taken over nature in most of California.

I'm lost in my pondering of the magnificence of undisturbed nature, when a tiny golden reflection from the setting sun catches my eye. I approach the trunk of an old oak tree, split and hollowed by a lightning strike years ago. The tree's bark has turned gray and brittle. I wouldn't have seen it without the low angle of the last sun rays, but here it is: a small speck of gold in the hollow of the dead tree.

"Vega, come over here. I think I've got something!" I shout.

She comes running over. Together we kneel in front of the old tree and brush aside the dry leaves piled up to conceal its opening.

"I can feel the folds of the Buddha's robes, his feet in the lotus position," she exclaims excitedly.

"He's in there. Shall we get him out?" I ask.

"No, we shouldn't touch him. He may have fingerprints on him. But we found him. We saved the Buddha." She is beaming at me.

Actually, *I* found him, I think, but I don't say it. Vega would just point out that my ego is talking. What about her ego?

"Okay, Vega, you go get the police, while I guard the Buddha."

She hurries back to the compound, while I sit watch in front of the hollow tree in the darkening forest. I hear faint noises from afar. People are going to dinner, but would anybody hear me, if I called for help? I doubt it. The fog creeps up on me, and I feel a chill running up my spine. Not just from the falling temperature. I'm alone in this part of the forest, with a murderer who knows my exact location. It's dark by now. No lights anywhere, not even a moon in the sky.

Close by I hear a breaking twig. Steps. Something brushes

against the chaparral. Something big. I try not to breathe, as if holding my breath would help. Silently I appeal to the Buddha in his hiding place, *It's you and me; both of our safety is at stake here. I don't know if you can do anything about it, but now would be the time....* The steps are coming closer. More than one pair of legs. *Vega, where are you?* The steps are so close now that I hear breath coming out in soft huffs. I need a weapon. Groping for a stick on the forest floor around me, I make too much noise. The steps halt in mid-motion. They know I'm here. Whatever happens, I'm not going down without a fight. I raise my stick. A sudden motion breaks through the underbrush, I jump up with a scream, ready to strike—and find myself face to face with a deer.

Lowering my weapon, I try to calm my beating heart. The deer looks as scared as I am.

"It's okay, everything's fine," I mumble. The deer takes one last look at me and bolts through the forest. Its white tail reflects in the darkness. The Buddha and I are both safe. I vaguely remember that the Buddha gave his first sermon after reaching enlightenment in a deer park. Deer were the first beings listening to him. That somehow seems significant.

"Greg," I hear Vega call. "Where are you?"

Flashlights and footsteps move in my direction.

"Over here, Vega!"

Vega and two police officers emerge from the darkness.

"There you are." She shines her light on me. "Everything okay?" she asks.

"Sure, the Buddha and I just had a nice little chat together."

~

8:00 P.M.

After another delicious dinner, considering it doesn't

include meat—brown rice, curried vegetables, crispy tofu, and Turmeric sauce—Vega and I amble over to the Zen-do.

The place is packed. Chairs were brought from the dining hall to accommodate everybody, and I'm grateful that the Ino assigns us to two of them. At least I don't have to sit cross-legged for the next hour or however long this talk is going to take. Instead, we sit comfortably next to each other and watch the students, guests, and monastics stream in.

They are a diverse bunch. There is a contingent of middle-aged African American women. I suppose they are Abbess Clarita's followers. They sit on pillows on the ground next to the raised platform of the Zen Master. Good for them. Better their knees than mine. A group of young kids with tattoos, black T-shirts, and a variety of piercings slink in and sit on the very last row of the platform. Several elderly men and women in practical, unflattering clothes bow to everybody in the correct order and take their pre-assigned seats. They look serious and somehow joyless, but what do I know? Maybe they are full of joy inside after years of practicing meditation.

I see Nomi crouching next to the drum and the temple bells and smile at her. But she doesn't respond. She has an important job, ringing the bell to announce the beginning and end of the *dharma* session. Finally, Osho Haku enters. The voices hush and silence settles over the Zen-do. He ascends the platform and takes his seat in the lotus position. Nomi rings the bell. Haku puts his palms together and bows. We all do the same, a sign of respect.

"Dear members of the *sangha*," he begins. "A tragic occasion brings us here tonight. The death of our beloved Abbess Clarita." Everybody bows again. "She was sitting on this very platform, doing what she had committed to do, practicing mindfulness and meditation. She died protecting our Buddha Amitabha, Lord of the West." He nods toward the empty pedestal, where the Buddha used to sit. "I am certain she died with his name on her lips and is now residing in the realm of the Western Paradise with Amitabha."

At least I know what he's talking about, but how did she get to the summit of Mount Fuji to enter?

"Dear members of the *sangha*, I have some good news for you. Abbess Clarita did not die in vain. Our precious Amitabha Buddha has been found. He was recovered this afternoon and will return to his pedestal soon, after the police have examined him for fingerprints and other traces of the crime. He has only suffered minor damage, which can be repaired relatively easily. We thank our lay members of the *sangha*, Vega and Greg Stern, for their help in this almost miraculous recovery."

Bows in our direction. We bow back, graciously, I hope.

"Let us remember the words of our great founder, Suzuki Roshi, which he spoke here in this hall on December fifth, 1967," Haku continues. "'Even though we die, if we know that all of us arose from nothingness; to die is to come back to the source of life.' Let us contemplate these words. Abbess Clarita returned to the source of life. She has moved on to a higher realm. And as soon as the police have finished with their forensic investigation and autopsy, her ashes will be returned and we will bury them next to the memorial of Suzuki Roshi up on the hill."

Many people in the audience are visibly moved, and I hear relieved gasps and long exhales.

"Suzuki Roshi said in the same talk that 'as long as we know what will happen to us after our death, there is nothing to be afraid of.' Abbess Clarita was not afraid. She died in a meditation pose here on this platform.

"I sit here, on her seat, only as a placeholder. In due time there will be an election to select a new abbot or abbess."

At least he's not trying to take over for good, even though he's not doing too badly.

"I know you all have many questions about what

happened and what is going to happen. You want to know how long you have to stay here, and what the police have found out so far. These questions are out of our control, since we have pledged to cooperate with the police in every way. I therefore asked Sergeant Rodriguez here tonight, to give you an update."

Rodriguez gets up from a chair by the entrance and walks over to stand next to the platform.

"Good evening, folks. First of all, our deep condolences for the loss of your abbess. Death occurred approximately between three and five o'clock yesterday morning. The cause of death seems to be strangulation. We are still conducting forensic tests. The autopsy will tell us more. We hope to return the body to you for cremation and funeral within three to five days."

A ripple goes through the audience at the mention of the upcoming funeral.

"In regard to the second crime, the theft of the Buddha statue, it has been recovered, as Osho Haku has already told you," Rodriguez continues. "The statue was haphazardly hidden, in a hollow tree, which barely concealed it and endangered the integrity of the sculpture. We are currently examining the statue for prints and other traces. We are treating the two crimes as connected."

Rodriguez shifts from one foot to the other. He looks around for reactions. I see Vega nodding in agreement. She probably provided the information about the Buddha statue's treatment to Rodriguez. I ponder the fact that the precious Amitabha Buddha wasn't very difficult to find.

"Now, no doubt, you want to know when you can go home. We hope to release you as soon as possible, but we need you to extend your stay by another day to assist in the investigation.

"There is no indication that anybody from the outside entered or left the monastery compound on the night of the incident. The road is very difficult to navigate, even during the daytime. Most likely the perpetrator is in our midst."

He pauses for effect and looks around. We all do the same, and I feel a shiver run down my spine. I have thought about the fact that the killer is one of us, but Rodriguez's words have really brought it home.

"We implore you not to leave the compound, to stay in groups, to not wander off by yourself. We'll do our best to protect you, and we don't want to alarm you unnecessarily, but use the utmost caution. Thank you and good night."

A somber procession files out of the Zen-do. People huddle together, pair up, look around furtively before disappearing into the darkness.

9:30 P.M.

Side by side, Vega and I walk back to our cabin.

"What did you think of Osho Haku's speech?" I ask.

"Traditional *dharma* stuff, non-attachment, death as a transition, honoring Abbess Clarita's sacrifice. What about you?"

"The part about Clarita giving her life for the Buddha sounded more like a Christian martyr to me. Plus, I heard Clarita and Haku were rivals in life."

"Where'd you hear that?"

"Here and there. Apparently he was resentful that she became abbess and not him."

"He was the senior monk."

We reach the cabin, but neither of us feels like going to bed yet.

"I brought us something," Vega says with a smile, "from the Carmel Valley supermarket."

"Let me guess: ham, prosciutto, salami?"

"Better. Wait here and I'll get it." She goes inside while I sit on the stoop and look up at the night sky through the branches of the trees. I hear her rummaging around in the cabin and then the sound of a plop. She comes back out carrying a bottle of merlot.

"You know me too well, Vega—a Russian River Valley merlot. My favorite." I try to give her a hug. She stiffens. She hasn't forgiven me yet.

"We have to drink from the bottle; there are no glasses."

"Not a problem. It'll just be like in the old days." This does turn out to be a bit like summer camp. First the joint snuck at the smoking site yesterday, now the wine from the bottle. I don't mind. It makes me feel young again. We continue down the path to a bench by the creek.

"I heard some incident in Haku's past prevented him from becoming abbot," I say after taking a big slug.

"You hear all the gossip, don't you?" Vega laughs. "He's well respected," she says, suddenly serious, and takes a big sip from the bottle.

"But he wasn't loved," I counter.

"You're right, Greg. Abbess Clarita was loved by everybody. She had wisdom and a generous heart. She also opened the Zen community to women, especially women of color."

"I was shocked when I first realized she was the abbess."

"Of course, she defied your expectations of a Zen Master."

"Haku fits the bill."

"Visually he does, but I'm not sure he can fill Abbess Clarita's shoes." Vega picks up a small pebble from the ground and throws it into the creek.

"What about this incident in his past?"

"Nothing was ever proven. It was his word against the girl's. As far as I'm concerned, he is still honorable."

"You believe him over the girl?" I say with more outrage than I feel, but I'd rather talk about Haku's relationship problems than Vega's and mine.

"It's his word against the word of a homeless junkie," she says and takes another swig.

"You surprise me, Vega. I thought you women stick

together." Why is she so forgiving with Haku, but not with me? "If he's so honorable, why did he lie about the construction?"

"What construction?"

"He told the police there was no construction going on here, when in fact several builders are at work by the yoga center."

"Why would Haku lie about something like that?" Vega sounds perplexed.

"Exactly."

Passing the bottle between us, we continue a bit farther on the path until the dense canopy overhead opens up to reveal a brilliant night sky, the ribbon of the Milky Way running across it like a silver river. We stare silently at the sparkling stars and avoid talking about the elephant in the room: the reason I am here.

2

D ay 3: 6:30 A.M.
A ray of sunshine tickles my nose and wakes me up. I sit up abruptly. What is a sun ray doing on my nose? The sun doesn't rises until after meditation. I reach over to Vega's futon next to mine. It's empty. She must have gone to morning meditation without me. Bless her heart. And I must've slept through the 5:30 morning bell.

How good it feels to lie here and stretch my legs! I'm starting to like this retreat a lot better since the monastic schedule went out the door. This pace is much more to my liking. Yesterday I was exhausted. The death of the abbess, Vega arriving, the retrieval of the Buddha—it all took its toll on me. Today, I need to do some investigating on my own.

I roll off the futon and pull on some clothes. The sun feels good on my back as I walk across the empty bridge. Small light reflections sparkle on the creek below. The courtyard in front of the dining hall is still empty. I enjoy a steaming cup of coffee by myself, before the little bell sounds and meditation lets out.

Vega finds me and I hand her a cup of coffee. She looks calm and composed.

"Thanks for letting me sleep in," I say.

"No point in forcing you to meditate if you don't want to and don't get anything out of it."

Coming from Vega that sounds too reasonable. I wonder what comes next.

"After breakfast I have to go to a meeting with the police and two detectives who just arrived."

"To talk about the Buddha."

"Yes. Sorry you can't come, Greg. You're still a suspect."

"I know. Just like everybody else. I was planning to go to the yoga center and the hot springs after breakfast."

"The yoga center?" Vega asks with raised eyebrows. "You want to do yoga?"

"I figure, I'll check it out. I'm here and can't leave the compound, so..."

Vega looks skeptical, but she lets it go.

9:30 A.M.

At breakfast, Rakesh, at our table, tells me that cooking is considered a form of meditation here. It's conducted with mindfulness like a spiritual practice. I guess that's why the food's so good.

We finish our oven-fresh muffins with homemade black-berry jam and butter, Vega goes to her meeting, and I amble over to the yoga center, just past the bathhouses.

Through the floor-to-ceiling windows, I see a group of women in tight yoga pants and sports bras stretching back-ward like cobras and hunching their bodies forward like cats. I admire their toned arms and tight butts and consider signing up for a class myself, when they suddenly dig their heads into the mats and lift one leg, then another, into a headstand. No, I could never do that. I'd kill myself. A yoga class is out.

But where's the construction? The yoga center looks well-built, solid. No cracks or repairs requiring construction work I can see. I walk a bit farther and see two men on a hill behind the center. Bill and another construction worker huddled together in front of some building equipment.

"Hey, Bill," I call out. He looks up as I walk up to meet him. "What are you guys doing here?"

"Surveying and soil testing. The ground is very brittle limestone here."

"Preparing for a new building?" I probe.

"Well." Bill shifts uncomfortably. "We're assessing the site for a new resort."

"Something a bit more comfortable than those redwood cabins. I like it."

"Those cabins are worse than rustic." Bill warms up to the topic. "No hot water, no shower, a basic toilet, and one of those thin mattresses on the floor."

"Futons," I offer.

"Whatever. We want to provide upscale accommodations for people to enjoy nature and take advantage of the healing hot springs. Some of them might be sick or elderly and couldn't even get up from those futons. And we want to put glass in the windows, not wax paper."

"Shoji screens."

He ignores me. "Folks could break their legs trying to use those primitive bathrooms."

"I hear you. I'm not a fan of those cabins either."

Bill looks at me and the trace of a smile appears on his face. "Your wife made you come here, right?"

I nod.

"Makes sense. You didn't come here because you wanted to."

"That pretty much sums it up."

"Okay. I gotta get back to work. See you at lunch."

I wander around a bit longer on the dry, brittle limestone soil. It hasn't rained in months. Looking for orange rope, I find a whole giant spool of it among the equipment. The rope has also been used to section off parts of the site. It looks just like the one on Clarita's lap.

12:00 noon

I decide to sit in the garden next to my cabin and read the *Wall Street Journal* I brought until lunch. It's three days old. I'd prefer to check my stock portfolio online, but I didn't bring my computer. There's no internet anyway. Maybe Nomi will come by. Instead, Vega shows up. She sits down on the bench beside me.

"How'd the meeting go?" I ask.

"It was inconclusive. They brought in this new detective, Abelli. He seems pretty sharp. We analyzed the whole issue of the Buddha. That's why I was there."

"Let's hear it."

"As we know, the Buddha was torn from his lotus throne and mandorla pretty roughly, seemingly in haste. That's why the wooden throne and the connecting wooden pegs were damaged."

"Okay, you already established that yesterday."

"Yes, but combined with the fact that the Buddha was hidden very poorly…"

"I think we did a pretty good job narrowing down where to look for him and finding him," I interrupt.

"Yes, but he was not even wrapped in a protective sheet or covering. He just sat on the bare ground in a hollow tree covered by a few leaves."

"So what?"

"Think about it. If we hadn't found him, he would have

been damaged badly. The art thieves didn't protect their loot very well."

"Okay, I see your point. They certainly didn't maximize their profit margin," I admit.

"Also, what was their exit plan? The parking area is guarded by police. They couldn't have gotten away."

"The police should search all cars for size, packing material, and other clues of intent to transport a valuable Buddha statue."

"They are," Vega says. "But as you know, most cars here, including yours, are SUVs with four-wheel drive and most have at least one blanket inside."

"So what's the conclusion?"

"Lack of motive. The thieves were unprepared; they didn't protect their asset and couldn't have sold the statue in the condition we found it in. The gold leaf was already beginning to peel. So the question is: Why did they do it, and how are the theft and the murder connected?"

"The thieves were interrupted by Clarita and had to rush the theft." I thought I had it figured out in my mind.

"I think the theft was improvised to cover up the murder, not the other way around. But it's up to the detectives to figure that out."

We hear the gong from the dining hall and I jump up. Lunch at 1:00 P.M. is late for me. I'm starving. "Let's continue talking after lunch," I suggest.

"Yes, we have to, because there are several implications."

1:00 P.M.

At lunch, which consists of fresh, crunchy whole-wheat bread, a vegetable frittata, and creamy asparagus and mushroom soup, we sit next to Bill. He's still wearing the same maroon polo shirt I saw at the construction site. It's pretty dusty. Must be his favorite outfit.

I introduce him to Vega; he smiles knowingly.

"I talked to Bill this morning, while you were at your meeting," I explain.

"Oh, how'd the yoga go?" she asks.

I ignore her question. "Bill is working on a building project behind the yoga center," I divert.

"What building project?" she asks.

"It's a resort center. A little more upscale than those 'rustic' cabins they are keeping us in now," I say.

"A resort?" Vega exclaims in alarm.

Bill tries to ease her concern, by telling her that they are only conducting soil testing and land surveying.

She's not having any of it. "The monastery could never afford, and would never condone, a resort complex."

"Sorry, folks, but I gotta go back to work," Bill says quickly. Then he gets up, grabs a piece of bread, and walks out.

Vega and I look at each other, dumbfounded at his abrupt departure.

2:00 P.M.

On the way back to our cabin across the creek, Vega says, "I'm very confused about this construction project."

"Maybe Osho Haku didn't lie after all. There is no construction, just survey and prep work being done. With proper accommodations, the center could expand their season instead of shutting down in the middle of September."

"I don't know, Greg. It doesn't sound right. This is a monastery, not a resort. They shut down for the winter to resume their serious meditation practice, without having to deal with all the guests."

"Think about it, Vega. With nice guest quarters they could attract tourists year round and make a lot of money."

"I don't think they want to attract tourists. The journey

and the stay here have to be a bit difficult, or else it wouldn't be rewarding. And it would attract the wrong crowd."

We've reached our cabin, but don't enter because there is no place to sit inside.

"Let's go sit by the creek," she says. "I have to talk to you about more important matters."

We walk to a shady bench overlooking the placidly gurgling brook.

"I have to go back today," she says.

"But you just got here."

"My job is done. The Buddha is back and I've told them all I could about its recovery. So, I'm leaving. I have to get back to my clients."

"All right, let's drive out together in my truck."

"No, Greg, you have to stay. I'm taking the supply truck again."

"What about my business? I can't even answer emails here."

"You have to stay at least a few more days."

"If I'm a suspect, you can keep an eye on me," I try, and wink at her.

No reaction. Vega looks at me stone-faced. "I can't and I won't," she finally says. "Remember the reason you're here in the first place?"

"Come on, I've shown remorse, and I've made a real effort. I think it's enough. I don't need any more punishment." I don't want to be reminded of the reason I'm here.

"It's not about punishment. I can forgive your transgression. It's just that you don't get it."

I take a deep breath to hide my irritation. "I don't get what?"

"You don't get women."

"That's unfair, Vega. We've been married over twenty-five years, and I pretty much know exactly what you're thinking."

Vega looks at me with raised eyebrows. "You have no idea what's going on in my mind, Greg."

"Try me." I'm so totally up for that challenge.

"Okay, what am I thinking now?"

"You're thinking that I don't appreciate you enough, and that I should be more considerate of your needs and feelings." I think I've nailed it, and look at her facial expression for confirmation—in vain.

"Totally wrong," she says immediately.

I don't believe her. That's exactly what she was thinking. "Then what?"

"I was thinking that you haven't even begun to explore your full potential."

"Excuse me, I'm running my own company and it's doing really well, thank you very much, affording us a pleasant lifestyle." I'm a bit put out by her statement. I have achieved a lot in my life. All these years I've worked hard to provide for my family and be successful.

"I don't mean financially, I mean your spiritual potential."

"Look, Vega, not everybody has to be a spiritual person." I'm so not going to talk about my spiritual potential.

"Why not? Why not try to expand our minds in the time we have on this earth?"

This is not a discussion I want to have. "What's wrong with me, Vega? Can't you love me the way I am?"

"Nothing's wrong with you, and I do love you—the way you are. But honestly, you haven't even started to figure out who you really are."

"I don't know what that's supposed to mean," I say, sulking.

"Exactly. That's the point."

She looks pretty smug, with a little superior smile on her lips.

"And I guess the only way to find out is meditation?"

"Right you are."

I expected her to say that, which proves that I know what she's thinking—but I don't rub it in. "You're not making this easy, Vega." Why can't I be enough for her, the way I am?

"It's not supposed to be easy. If it were easy, it wouldn't be worth very much."

"Another one of these Zen sayings. Probably something Mr. Suzuki said." I've just about heard enough Suzuki quotes to last me a lifetime.

"Yes, Suzuki Roshi did say that. But it's also common sense."

"Not really," I sigh. "You know, if I didn't love you, I wouldn't do this."

"I know." She pauses.

At this point she is supposed to tell that she loves me too. But instead she says, "If you want, I'll notify your clients."

"No, I'll do it myself, when I get back." I'm imagining the dramatic reports I will be able to make telling them about the murder investigation.

Vega smiles. "I thought so. I have to go—, the supply truck won't wait. They have to be back before dark." She kisses me on the forehead and gets up. "See you in a week, or so," she says and walks to the cabin to grab her bag.

I stay on the bench and listen to the creek gurgling over the rocks.

No answers there.

3:30 P.M.

Vega is gone and there is nothing to do. I lie on the futon in my cabin, but I'm not tired. No wonder: I remember sleeping in this morning. I hear the wooden clacks from the Zen-do, calling to the afternoon sitting session. Maybe I'll go. I have nothing else to do.

On my way to the Zen-do I think about what Vega just said, that I haven't even begun to explore who I really am.

That's unfair. I know exactly who I am, and I'm fine with it. I'm basically a good person, a good provider, successful in my profession. I made a little mistake, but compared to what many others do, nothing major. Vega is making too much out of this. I'm pretty comfortable in my own skin, and I don't see anything wrong with the way I am. I don't have a hole in my soul.

4:00 p.m.

Sitting on my pillow on the meditation platform, I feel the familiar restlessness and annoyance. But the quality of the feeling is different. Only a few students sit at this time of day. Nomi rings the bell and all is quiet. The Zen-do feels more casual than in the morning. Less pressure. I'm also wide awake. More noises enter from outside, people walking and talking on the path in in the courtyard. How inconsiderate of them. Don't they realize some of us want to meditate? I have to smile at my own indignation. Normally I would be the one out there, walking and talking. But whom should I talk to? Vega left.

I breathe slowly and listen to the birds outside. Filtered light comes in through the shoji screens. I worry about how long I have to sit here. I get tired of thinking about the time. Instead, I take a few breaths, resigned to just sitting it out.

Suddenly a warm energy flows from my feet along my spine to the top of my head like an air bubble in a soda bottle. I didn't see it coming, didn't expect it, didn't try for it to happen.

Is this supposed to happen? As soon as I have this thought, the energy evaporates, the bubble bursts. I remind myself not to think so much, but that's thinking too. So I just breathe and become aware of my feet below me and the mat that holds them, and the wooden platform below. My mind sort of expands to take it all in: how the cushion is made of cotton, which grew in the earth, like the trees that made the wood, and how both needed sunlight and water, just as I do, and the people who picked the cotton and cut the tree and made this platform and built this temple, they all needed water, and without rain none of this would exist, and I wouldn't exist; and the rain wouldn't exist without clouds, and the clouds wouldn't exist without the sun and the winds that wrap them around this planet. All of this had to come together and work in unison so I could sit here at this place at this moment.

My mind almost pops with the enormity of it all. I feel so incredibly important and blessed, and at the same time minuscule and completely unimportant, just a tiny link in the huge, interconnected universe. I see myself in the center as if from high above, but also as a part of it, observing and creating the moment simultaneously.

Pling, the little bell rings. I startle. We just began this meditation, but I hear the people next to me shifting, bowing, and getting up. I open my eyes and blink. I guess it's over. Is it possible that forty-five minutes just went by?

I get up and turn around to see Nomi smiling at me. I smile back, still dazed by what has happened. At the shoe shelves, we meet and walk off together.

"Did you have a good meditation?" she asks.

"It was great. I didn't expect this, I wasn't even trying…"

"That's when the best insights happen, when you don't expect anything, and don't try too hard."

"This just about blew my mind."

"In his book *Zen Mind—Beginner's Mind,* Suzuki Roshi says 'in the beginner's mind there are many possibilities, but in the expert's there are few.'"

"Nomi, what does Zen try to teach?"

"Zen doesn't teach anything. It just points the way."

"The way to what?" I ask, assuming that was another one of Suzuki Roshi's sayings.

"Your way." She turns off toward the kitchen, leaving me with another riddle.

I wonder if that's what Vega has been talking about. I really don't understand Zen. It's out of my league. From my limited experience, it looks like a serious pursuit for very serious people who devote years to sitting in meditation, and in the end they are still very serious. I don't see the joy in it.

But this meditation today was more than joyful. I have no idea what it meant or what happened, but it felt great.

I think about Nomi, and the hole in her soul. Maybe Zen worked for her. She's not drinking anymore, and she seems to know something I don't. Maybe Zen is as good a way to fill that hole as any. Who am I to judge?

3

D ay 4: 5:30 A.M.
I hear the bell ringer and get up right away. I'm eager to experience that mind-boggling state again, where I'm everywhere at once.

By now I'm an old hat at the etiquette. I bow and shuffle like a pro to my seat assigned by the Ino and stare at the white wall with a pleasant smile, as if it were a movie screen and the show was about to start.

The final bell announcing the start of meditation rings and then it begins: the interminable, unbearable, torturous, never-ending forty-five minutes of *zazen*. My legs fall asleep and are so numb, I fear they'll have to be amputated. My mind is crawling with ants and my thoughts jump around like toddlers on a preschool playground.

When the final bell rings, I crawl off the platform. My seat neighbor helps me to my feet for the final bow. Devastated, I limp across the path to the courtyard and pour myself a desperately needed cup of coffee.

Nomi sits down next to me on the stonewall with her cup

of tea. I'm glad for her company. She's the only one who understands what I'm going through.

"It didn't go so well this morning?" she asks kindly. I love the cute dimples in her cheeks when she smiles.

"Terrible. It was the worst."

"Because you had expectations," she says. "It usually happens like that. Yesterday, you had beginner's mind. You were open, and the moment unfolded for you. Take it as a gift."

"Is it coming back?"

"It all depends on your state of mind." She puts her hand on my arm in a friendly gesture.

I'm disproportionally moved. It feels so good. What's happening to me? Have I been so deprived, I'm turning into a marshmallow? A girl puts her hand on my arm and I melt like butter in a frying pan.

Nomi smiles and gets up. "See you in the garden," she says and walks off.

9:00 A.M.

At breakfast I sit next to one of Clarita's followers. She introduces herself as Cora Howard from Los Angeles. I tell her my name is Greg. We talk about the late abbess and Cora tells me how Clarita changed her life, while we chow down on flatbreads with honey and fresh fruit. Cora has a good appetite.

"Clarita taught me about freedom," Cora says. "Before I knew her, I didn't feel I had any choices. My life was just suffering, with no way out. I had no control. I was a single mom, with two little kids, working two jobs just to pay the rent on a rat-infested dump in southeast LA."

"How'd you meet her?"

"A friend at church told me about this Zen Master who looked like me. I didn't believe her, but there she was, at the

Zen Center in LA."

"How'd she change your life?"

Cora pauses and I look at her face, shaped by a life of hard work and struggle.

"Clarita taught me that my limitations were just in my mind. I know, it doesn't sound like much, but for me it was a revelation."

I like Cora; she's very down to earth. "So now you meditate every day?"

"If and when I can. I still have the kids and my jobs. I came with a group for a weeklong retreat, to have time for ourselves, to meditate and to attend teachings by Clarita."

"Her loss must be horrible for you. I'm so sorry."

"We're devastated. She was the one we looked up to. She gave us strength, and now she's gone. I feel like it all came crumbling down."

I almost say something like "but you still have this place here, you can still meditate, and remember, it's all in your mind," but I bite my tongue. Who am I to spout such trite and shallow comfort? Maybe I'm getting wiser. Instead, I put my hand on her arm in a gesture of empathy, I hope.

Cora looks at me, looks at my hand, smiles lopsidedly, and gently removes my hand from her arm. She's not moved. Oh well.

"Don't worry about us, honey. We're tough. You gotta be tough growing up as a black woman in southeast LA. Clarita, she was the toughest of all."

I nod encouragingly, careful not to touch her anymore.

"Clarita never made it a secret that she was a survivor of sexual assault, and her son was killed in a drive-by shooting by rival gang members."

"Oh my God," I exclaim.

"Her son's father was a gang member, but her son refused to join, at Clarita's insistence. So they shot him. At the time Clarita still went to a Baptist church, but I suppose the church couldn't provide the answers she needed. Was it God's will that her son was killed? An innocent boy of fourteen? Do you have children, Mr....?"

"Stern."

"Mr. Stern, do you have children?"

"Two sons. They're both grown now." I don't tell her to call me Greg. I have a feeling she prefers the formality. I'm proud of myself for being so sensitive and observant. Vega should be impressed.

"Then you can imagine what it means to lose a child. You never get over that."

I nod. "Is that when Clarita turned to Zen?"

"She did more than that. She turned to the police. She gave them the information to take out the entire gang leadership, including their drug-dealing business and their prostitution ring."

"Wow, how brave of her."

"Obviously, after the trial Clarita had to disappear. She had a huge target on her chest. She changed her name and came here. The perfect place to disappear."

"So she did have enemies."

"That she did, but I can't imagine they found her here."

"Hmm, but it is a possibility. You told the police this story, I assume?"

"I did, honey. Listen, I gotta go. I have to call in to work and talk to my kids. I hope they let us go soon. I gotta get back to my life."

"Good luck with everything," I say as Cora leaves.

It sounds like Clarita was an inspiring and courageous person. Maybe I should read one of her books.

10:00 A.M.

The temple gong outside the dining hall summons us with resonating vibrations. I'm confused. Breakfast is over—

we just finished. People stream into the courtyard where Osho Haku and Detective Abelli stand at the top of the stairs overlooking the court, like they have something important to say.

"Dear members of the *sangha*," Osho Haku begins. "Detective Andy Abelli, who has taken over the investigation, has an important announcement to make." He steps back.

Abelli looks much too stylish for this environment. He wears a well-cut gray Italian suit and elegant leather loafers. He's not getting far in those shoes out here.

"Thank you for your attention," he says and rakes his hands through his slightly-too-long brown hair. "I have good news and bad news. The good news is that the expedited autopsy of your abbess, Clarita, is completed. Her ashes will be released for her funeral tomorrow."

A sigh of relief ripples through the attendees.

"The bad news, however, is that one member of this community is missing. Brother Jacob was last seen yesterday evening at dinner. When he didn't appear for meditation this morning, Osho Haku and the...the monk who assigns the seats..."

"...the Ino..." Haku inserts the correct word.

"Yes, the Ino, got worried. He sent a student to his room. Brother Jacob's bed looks unused. Has anybody seen him since five o'clock last night?"

Silence. People look around, look at each other. Heads are shaking.

"Nobody? Does anybody have information about his whereabouts? Where he was going?"

Haku says, "Brother Jacob has lived here for over five years; he's one of the most established and reliable members of our *sangha* and he is our office manager."

He had full access to the only computer and phone here, I think. How completely could he be trusted, and is his disappearance connected to his position as the office manager?

Abelli perks up. He's obviously made the same connection. "Does he monitor the phone calls?"

"No, but he's in the same room," Haku clarifies.

"So he could overhear telephone conversations?"

"Theoretically, yes, but he would never eavesdrop." Haku seems to have full confidence in Jacob.

"Are there any other telephones here?"

"No," Haku says. "Privacy is limited here by design."

Abelli scrunches up his nose at this piece of information. It's going to make his job a lot harder, trying to conduct confidential interviews. I have to admit I'm not a fan of the open-door, full-transparency, no-privacy policy.

"We'll launch a search party with the help of the forest rangers in the area. As I understand, Jacob is an avid hiker. I want to remind you, if anybody knows Brother Jacob's favorite trail, or if anybody spoke to him last night, please come and talk to us. This also underlines the importance of staying within the compound. Does anybody have any questions or comments?"

Several hands go up. "When can we go home?" comes a question from the group.

"We have to ask you to extend your stay for a day or two. The investigation depends on your availability."

"But you know where to find us," someone shouts out.

"We need to conduct another round of interviews due to Jacob's disappearance before people leave. I apologize for the inconvenience, but we need your cooperation. Any other questions?"

Of course Abelli knows it was one of us.

"What were the results of Abbess Clarita's autopsy?" I ask.

"The body of the abbess showed signs of strangulation. I'm sorry I can't get into the details, as you will surely understand."

I remember the orange rope on her lap, when we found her sitting on the platform just a few mornings ago.

A murmur of subdued voices ripples through the crowd.

"What about the Buddha? When is he coming back?" someone calls out.

"We're still testing the statue for fingerprints and other traces, but I am optimistic that the Buddha will be back in time for the funeral tomorrow. Thank you for your attention, and please stay within the compound."

Abelli retreats and Haku steps up onto the stone wall separating the courtyard form the main path. His simple dark robes form a sharp contrast to Abelli's designer suit.

"We are planning the funeral service for Abbess Clarita tomorrow at three o'clock at the Zen-do, followed by a procession up to the Suzuki Roshi memorial. You are all invited." He bows deeply.

11:00 A.M.

The situation is definitely heating up. Now we have a missing person. I thought I was coming to a peaceful place, but instead I encounter one disaster after another. At the office/gift store I buy Clarita's book. I get the last one. No wonder people are reading: there is no other form of entertainment. While browsing, I notice the *Zen Mountain Retreat Cookbook* and decide to buy a copy of it. When I get back home, I will replicate some of the recipes for Vega. She'll love that. I take the books to the garden bench to read, hoping that Nomi will show up. She does and sits down next to me.

"What're you reading?" she asks.

"Clarita's book on freedom." I hope this impresses her.

"I heard it's very good. I haven't read it."

"She quotes your founder, Suzuki. Listen to this: 'Zen in its essence is the art of seeing into the nature of one's being, and it points the way from bondage to freedom.'"

"I like that."

"I don't understand it. If Zen is all about freedom, then why are we confined to this monastery and why are there so many rules about pretty much everything?"

"It's about freedom of mind, not freedom of the body," she laughs.

Right. I figured she'd say something like that, and decide to change the subject.

"What do you think happened to Brother Jacob? How well do you know him?"

"Not well. He's very quiet. Always friendly, always doing his job, working, taking care of things. I'm really upset about his disappearance. He's one of those people without an ego, more concerned about others than himself."

"Wow, is that really possible?"

"Actually, that's what it's all about."

"Do you know his background? Where'd he come from?"

"He was here long before me. I think he joined the monastery when he was fairly young. He told me that he always wanted to be part of a spiritual community. I hope they find him."

"Me too. What about Clarita? I heard she was here on a witness protection program," I say.

She laughs. "You hear all the gossip, don't you? Maybe at first she was here for protection, but she embraced this place. She wasn't hiding. She wanted to be here."

"Do you think someone from the old street gang found her here?"

"And posed as a retreat guest?" She laughs. "An LA gang member sitting *zazen* every morning at six o'clock? Hard to imagine."

"And eating vegetarian food, wearing loose neutral clothing, abstaining from alcohol and electronic devices?" We laugh together picturing it.

"They could have sent someone," I consider.

"A hit man sharing our dining and meditation hall? He would have to be a very good and patient actor with no exit plan."

I shrug. "I don't feel it's out of the question, and it didn't have to be a man."

Nomi looks at me, wide-eyed. "Tomorrow is the funeral. You should come," she says. "It's a simple, moving ceremony. Clarita's brother is coming from LA to attend."

"What should I wear for the occasion?" I ask.

"White clothes would be perfect, but black's fine. And you can bring flowers."

"Where would I get flowers?"

"Look around you. Right here in this garden. You can pick some."

I look at the pink zinnias, orange California poppies, and blue mountain lupines shivering in the light breeze. A carpet of colors, overflowing their beds.

"I'll be there. It's not like I have any other pressing engagements."

She smiles. "You do, actually. Your pressing engagement is right here, right now."

I look at her, not sure what she means. Is this just another Zen saying, or does she imply something else about our engagement right here, right now? We're sitting close, our legs are touching. I think maybe there's a message there. I gently put my hand on her knee.

She looks at me and then at her knee, with my hand on it. After a short hesitation, she takes my hand and moves it away from her leg softly. "That's not what I meant. Your appointment is with yourself and the present moment."

"We're friends, right?" I lean toward her.

"Greg, we are not friends. You're a guest. You'll leave in a few days. I live here. I'm going to be a nun. I'm going to shave my head and give up all attachments."

"But until then, we can smoke a joint and have some fun."

"You've got it all wrong. Having fun is not the purpose." She gets up and steps back a pace.

"You've been my guide, Nomi. I'm all alone here. I don't know how anything works without you."

"This is not about you. You're taking yourself too seriously. Most people, especially men, overestimate their own importance. You have to let go of your ego. And you have to let go of me." She gets up and turns on her heel. Before she leaves, I think I see a tear running down her cheek. Is she mad at me or is something else going on?

What the heck did I do? How'd that go south so quickly? What'd she get so huffy about? It's not like I tried to kiss her. These Zen people are way too uptight. She totally overreacted. I'm doing my freaking best here. It's not easy with all these rules and expectations. And why is it okay for her to put her hand on me, but not the other way around?

2:00 P.M.

I'm upset after the confrontation with Nomi. At lunch, I barely notice what I put in my mouth. Afterward, I walk over to the bathhouse to relax in the hot tub. I enter through the men's side. The indoor spa for the hot springs is empty, but through the glass I see the guys in the natural stone outdoor tub. Rakesh is there; Bill; Hans Becker, who's Bill's colleague; and a young kid with long hair and tattoos. The steam is rising to the beech trees above, and the familiar rotten-eggs sulfur smell snakes its way into my nostrils. I take off my clothes and open the sliding door to the deck. Over the babbling creek below, I hear the voices of the guys discussing Jacob's disappearance. I join them.

"How did Jacob get away? He's always in the office," Rakesh says.

"I guess he disappeared after dark." I shift on the rocks in the tub, trying to get comfortable.

"It gets dark early now, at the end of summer," says the young kid.

"Who are you?" Bill asks bluntly.

"Dylan. I'm a volunteer. I help in the kitchen in exchange for room, board, and meditation time."

"They let you use the spa during work hours?" Rakesh asks.

Like me, he is paying dearly for the privilege to be here and obviously is not overly excited to mingle with the help.

"Normally we're supposed to use the spa before eight A.M., but with the murder and everything, the schedule has gotten all mixed up..."

"Have you heard what the police are planning to do?" I ask. If he wants to mingle with us, at least he can divulge some information.

"They're searching the trails, with the help of forest rangers," Dylan says, but we know this already.

"I've hiked a lot of them. Very rugged and treacherous. Jacob wouldn't get very far in the dark," Rakesh says. His eye is twitching again. The stress must get to him.

"I hope Abelli brought another pair of shoes and pants," I say to change the subject, imagining Abelli navigating the rugged trails in his Italian loafers.

Everybody laughs.

"We had to lend him some clothes and hiking boots," Dylan says. "They don't fit as well as his Armani suit, but they'll get him on the trail."

"Did you hear anything else?"

"I heard them discussing the abbess's autopsy. She actually died of a heart attack, not the strangulation. They think the shock of the intruder, the theft of the Buddha, and the attack on her caused her heart to give out." Dylan enjoys the attention. Doesn't everybody? I think we all like to be noticed, men and women alike.

"Ahhh, the plot thickens," Bill coos.

"Did they find fingerprints on the Buddha?" I ask.

"All smudged, or destroyed by the moisture," Dylan declares with authority.

"You think Jacob overheard something?" I look up into the green canopy above, as if searching for surveillance devices.

"And got murdered for it?" Rakesh shoots back.

"It's a motive…" I consider.

"Then we're all suspects. We've all made our calls in the office and were overheard by Jacob."

"It doesn't exactly narrow down the playing field," Hans admits. "If they don't find Jacob soon, they'll check all our phone records."

"I just called my boss and told him about the delay," Rakesh says.

"I had to notify DB Builders. Dick Baxter wants us to finish up here ASAP. It got a bit heated." Bill smacks his flat hand into the water for emphasis. Water drops splash up and land on my nose.

"What's he like, your employer?" I ask him.

"Dick Baxter? Very type-A personality. He has to get his way. Always on to the next, big project."

"And he wants this resort here done right away," I guess.

"It's complicated and a bit controversial," Bill says with finality.

We shift in the warm waters and watch the steams rise into the air. The sun has come out and together with the water vapor creates a shifting curtain of light.

I make a mental note to call Vega, to tell her about Jacob's disappearance and ask her to look into DB Builders. Something sounds fishy there.

4

Day 5: 6:00 A.M.
I'm sitting on my mat in the Zen-do when Nomi rings the bell. I really don't want to see her right now. Fortunately I'm facing the wall. I feel bad about what happened between us. A misunderstanding, obviously. I thought we had a nice connection going, the two of us. I hate for her to be upset with me. Without her smile and occasional insights, my stay here feels tedious and pointless. All kinds of things swirl through my head. I feel unproductive and lost. I love the food, but it's served at inconvenient times, and Clarita's book is not exactly easy reading. I resent being held captive here. I should be working and I need exercise.

My anger and frustration are going round and round in my mind until they lose steam and I just sit there exhausted, but calmer, until the final bell rings and meditation is over.

11:00 A.M.
I'm lounging around, waiting for the funeral. From the smoking spot I see the tree where we found the Buddha,

roped off with yellow crime-scene tape. From here I witness the arrival of a big black SUV in the parking area. The doors open and out climb two black and two white men in dark suits and sunglasses. Clarita's brother and the FBI? Or are they federal marshals from witness protection? They look out of place. Their dress shoes slip on the gravel road, as they walk toward the monastery gate in formation. I try to guess which one is Clarita's brother. He must be the largest of the four. They all straighten their jackets and step through the Japanese-style wooden gate. Now they are in a different world that has nothing in common with the place they came from.

I think about the collision of these worlds: the Zen community and southeast LA; federal marshals and this remote spiritual monastery, which has never seen a crime before. My busy world of private security and this place where space and time are always in the present also seem incompatible. Before coming here, I didn't even know places like this existed.

3:00 P.M.

The *sangha* assembles in the Zen-do for the service before the procession up the hill to Suzuki Roshi's memorial. The students and volunteers brought in chairs from the dining hall and I gratefully take a seat in one of them. At least I don't have to sit cross-legged for the next hour. Clarita's brother, as the guest of honor, sits next to the platform where she died. Next to his chair stands the other African American man from the van. During a brief interaction with Clarita's brother, I see rows of reflecting gold and silver teeth caps blinking in his mouth. Is he a friend? A relative? The two white men— federal agents, marshals?— stand wide-legged in a posture of strength on either side of the entrance, hands in front on top of each other.

The Buddha is back. He sits on his pedestal as if nothing ever happened. Unflappable. I guess that's his claim to fame.

Nomi sits on her pillow next to the temple bell and the gong. I'm not looking at her.

Haku enters last, as the residing Zen Master. He bows in front of the altar, which is nothing more than a polished piece of wood still showing the bark of the tree it came from. In front of it leans a picture of Clarita in her monastic robes, head shaved. A bowl of rice, water, burning incense sticks, and a vase with white flowers complete the arrangement. Simple. The urn with her ashes stands on the pedestal next to the Buddha.

The wooden sticks clack, and everyone bows, palms together. Haku speaks.

"Dear members of the *sangha*, we will make offerings to the Buddha and give thanks for his safe return. We are assembled here in gratitude for Abbess Clarita's life, which we were privileged to share for a few short years. I want to introduce Clarita's brother, Michael, and thank him for coming here and honoring us with his presence."

I see a frown on Michael's face. It's not like he came here for festivities.

The monastics begin to chant in Japanese and I let the sound wash over me. It lulls me into a pleasant state of numbness.

I see Clarita's brother scanning the faces of his sister's followers, sitting on cushions on the floor. Does he know any of them?

After the chanting, Haku asks Michael to speak. He stands straight, tall and imposing. Looks around the hall.

"I have never been here before," he begins. "My sister Dorothy disappeared from LA and came here. I only knew she found refuge in a Zen community, for her own safety. I didn't know what a Zen community was, until today. And I didn't know where it was located. Once in a while, I received messages from her, without a return address. She wrote that she was happy and safe." He looks around at the audience and raises his voice. "And two years later she is dead!" he shouts.

People flinch. This hall has never heard such a loud and angry tone. So Clarita's real name was Dorothy.

"One of you killed her! We, her family, made the ultimate sacrifice, giving her up to save her life, because she had saved many. Countless young girls and boys would have ended up in a life of crime, drugs, and prostitution without her. I myself was able to transform my life because of her. With her support, I was able to move out of our neighborhood and get a college education." He pauses and balls his fists.

"What did you do to protect her? I accuse you. One of you is the ultimate traitor. I'm looking straight into your eyes. Which one of you was it?"

People twitch and wiggle in their seats. This is hard to listen to. A bit too intense, even for my taste.

"They tell me she died protecting a Buddha. Is that supposed to comfort me? She died protecting a piece of wood?"

I look at Haku. He looks stricken. I can imagine this is a low blow for him, but I can also understand Michael's point of view. The Buddha statue doesn't mean anything to him. I hear a sob from one of Clarita's followers. Did any of them know Clarita in her former life?

"This will be the first and last time I come here. I wasn't allowed to see my sister, for her and my protection. All I could do was trust that she was safe. You have broken that trust, and I will never forgive or forget." He turns abruptly and sits down, glaring at the assembled audience.

Wow, what's there to say after that? I don't envy Haku having to respond to this speech.

Haku rises. He looks calm and composed. I can only imagine the discipline this requires.

"Thank you, Michael, for coming here and sharing your thoughts," he begins.

Sharing your thoughts? That was more like hurling accusations. Honestly, I don't blame Michael; his pain is very raw.

"We understand and share your grief and your love for your sister," Haku continues. "We elected her as our abbess, our leader, and I am sure all of us would have done anything to protect her. Do any of you want to share your memories of Clarita at this time, before we conclude this service and begin the procession to the memorial site to lay her ashes to rest?"

One of Clarita's followers, handsome African American woman of about thirty-five, gets up and walks to the platform. She pointedly stands on the other side from Michael.

"My name is Mary, and I met Clarita at the Zen Center in LA, before she came here. I don't know what made me walk through those doors on Normandy Ave that day in late summer. I think it was pure exhaustion. I just wanted to get out of the heat and the noise and smell of the street for a little bit. It was cool and quiet inside. I figured they'd throw me out any minute. But then Clarita came up to me. She looked like me, except older and completely calm. She offered me a cold glass of water and an attentive ear. We talked for over an hour." Mary pauses, fighting with her emotions. She has an Egyptian profile and expressive eyes. After regaining her composure, she continues. "I couldn't believe someone was taking the time to listen to me. I was living on the street at the time. Mostly on Skid Row, doing drugs and selling myself for the next hit. Clarita took me in, and gradually the fog in my mind cleared. I owe her my life, and my health, and my sanity. I owe her everything." She breaks down in sobs and hurries back to her seat.

I'm almost moved to tears. This is turning out to be a very dramatic funeral service. Not what I expected from a Zen gathering, but nothing here really turns out to be according to my expectations.

The other women in Mary's group comfort and hug her. Haku gets up again to take control. I think we've had about all the emotional outbursts we can handle. Sure enough, Haku doesn't ask for another testimonial. He bows to the altar and makes an offering of rice, water, and a white flower to Clarita's image. More chanting begins and the people in the audience, who know what to do, form a long line, snaking toward the altar, where they also deposit offerings of rice and flowers.

I wait them out, clutching my flowers from the garden.

Finally everybody has paid tribute. The procession, led by the Ino carrying the urn, begins to form. Haku comes next, inviting Michael to join him, followed by the rest of the monastics, volunteers, and guests. The federal agents and police stand around uncomfortably, staying beside the procession, trying to keep an eye on everybody.

On the way up the trail to the memorial site, I walk next to Cora.

"That was intense," I comment.

"A bit too tense," she says. "I never met Michael before, but I'm sorry he's so full of anger and accusation. His sister wouldn't have liked that."

"Too bad she couldn't teach him some equanimity," I say.

"They never really saw each other again, after the trial. For their own protection."

"I guess so. Do you know Mary and the other women in your group pretty well?" I ask.

"We try to meditate together once a week, but usually it's more like once a month, what with work and kids and life. But we try to spend a little time together when we meet; drink tea; support each other."

I nod.

"One of the women is kinda new to this. She still seems pretty lost. Life is hard out there."

"How new?" I ask.

"About six weeks, I'd say."

"How long does it take before you get the hang of this Zen thing? I'm pretty new at it myself."

She laughs. "I know, honey, it's pretty obvious. Well, this Zen thing, as you call it, pretty much takes a lifetime."

"I was afraid you'd say that," I admit.

"You don't seem the type to seek out this kind of retreat." She looks at me appraisingly.

"Because I'm not desperate? Because I don't have a hole in my soul?"

"Yeah, something like that." She smiles.

"The new woman, how desperate is she?"

"Priscilla? I'd say on a scale from one to ten, she's about a nine. I hope she makes it. Not everybody can escape a life on the streets. I take it you don't live in LA?"

We have to slow down and stop talking, because the dirt path leading up to the memorial is getting steep. We pass through a weathered old torii gate, which frames the forest path behind like a painting.

The beginning of the procession has arrived and people fan out around Suzuki Roshi's memorial, a simple stone marker.

A small hole in the ground has been prepared to hold Clarita's ashes. The site is peaceful, with a panoramic view of the valley below and the village of the monastery buildings and guesthouses. A nice place to rest, forever.

After a bit more chanting and bowing, Haku begins to pour the ashes into the hole.

"No!" Clarita's brother shouts, grabbing Haku's arm to stop him. "Can't you leave anything of her? Can't you allow anything to remain?"

If these were the ashes of my sister, I'd be shouting too.

Haku looks at him undisturbed. "Michael," he says calmly, "your sister was a Zen Master. This is what she wanted. She's one with the universe now. Her ashes are becoming part of this earth, this mountain. She rests right next to our founder, Suzuki Roshi, who said, 'Life is a period of itself, death is a period of itself. They are like winter and spring. We do not call winter the future spring, nor spring the future summer.' Please respect the wishes of your sister." He continues pouring the ashes.

"I don't know what that's supposed to mean. I don't care about your fucking universe—I want my sister back." Michael's friend holds onto his arm to restrain him.

Even though I understand Michael's anger, I have to respect Haku's composure. All the monastics show great poise, actually. The police stand at the periphery and observe the proceedings. I glance over at Clarita's followers and try to guess which one is Priscilla.

After the ashes have been poured into the hole, another line forms and each person places a rock on the small earthen mound, which is now Clarita's resting place. Since I already brought the flowers and have been clutching them the entire time, I place them on the mound. A rock would've been a lot easier.

5

Day 6: 5:30 A.M.
      I wake up to the morning bells and a downpour. The bells sound wobbly in the rain and water drips down into my cabin through the shoji screens in the windows. I have to move the futon into the middle of the cabin, out of reach. I peek out the window and see the bell ringer walk by in a rain poncho, dripping wet. Rain is good, I think, remembering complaints about drought, dying trees, and fire danger.

Without rain gear, I hurry to the Zen-do in my sweatpants and flip-flops. The creek under the bridge has grown into a rushing river. Let's see how the meditation hall holds up in the rain. Thoughtfully, the retreat administration has provided towels by the shoe shelves. They don't want us to drip on their precious wooden platforms.

On my cushion, I listen to the rain and smell the damp air through the open windows. It's a warm end-of-summer rain, and I cherish the moisture in the air after the long, dry days and the sound of the raindrops pattering on the roof. The various emotional outbursts at the funeral yesterday pass in front of my inner eye. Michael and his entourage drove back to the city last night. Many of the guests are planning to leave today. They have given their second statements, the funeral is over, and the police can't hold them any longer. I wish I could leave as well. I need to get back to Vega and work and to the real world.

From previous experience, I know that thinking about work makes these forty-five minutes even more painful, so I try to return to the moment, my breath, and the pattering of the rain.

Have I learned anything in my time here? Nomi would say Zen doesn't teach anything, it just points the way. So, have I found anything? Not yet. I really want to find out who killed Clarita.

7:00 A.M.

After meditation we trudge across the path to the court-yard, which has turned into a mud field. They have opened the dining hall early, so we snatch our coffee, shed our shoes at the entrance, and slip inside, out of the downpour. Break-fast isn't ready yet, but we sit at the tables nursing our hot drinks.

Haku and Abelli enter and stand in the doorway. Haku brought a little bell to get our attention. Abelli wears jeans, boots, and a rain jacket. Quite an adjustment.

"Good morning," Haku says casually, unlike his usual formal self. "We have a bit of bad news."

"Not more bad news," a guest heckles him.

"The rain has caused a major mudslide on the only access road, making it impassable. So, at present, we are cut off from the outside world." Haku has a big smile on his usually stern face. Is he feeling cheerful about being cut off from the outside world?

"Noooo," a moan erupts from the assembled group.

Abelli takes over. "The forest rangers are working on the damage, but as you see it's still raining hard, which makes it very dangerous to navigate the mountain. We're very sorry, but you will have to postpone your departures."

"So what happens next?" Hans Becker, Bill's burly blond colleague, calls out.

"We have to wait until the rain stops and the road can be repaired," Haku answers. "This has happened before."

"How long is it going to take?" Cora asks.

"It depends on the weather. We may have to cut down on provisions, since the supply truck can't get through either."

"Rationing?" I gasp. The food is the only highlight here.

"Hopefully it won't take longer than a few days. We have enough supplies, so don't worry, you won't starve."

"What a relief," someone shouts sarcastically. Haku ignores the comment and smiles pleasantly.

"In the meantime stay safe, stay dry, and stay calm," Abelli adds.

"What about Jacob? Have you found him?" another guest calls out.

Abelli frowns. "This downpour has complicated the search. The rangers are focused on reopening the road. It's extremely dangerous to navigate the trails and we are surrounded by thousands of acres of national forest. But I've been told that Jacob was a skilled naturalist. It's possible he found a dry spot and is just waiting for the rain to stop, before he returns."

"Did he take any of his gear, or provisions?" Nomi asks.

Haku shakes his head sadly.

Of course, after this announcement the noise level rises exponentially as people vent about these new circumstances and speculate about Jacob's whereabouts.

I see Cora and the four other women from the LA *sangha* sitting at a table together. Three of them talk loudly and with great animation. The youngest, however, sits apart. Her face looks haggard, almost gray. Absently, she stares into her teacup. I sidle up to the table and sit next to her. This must be Priscilla.

"What an inconvenience," I begin. "We're stuck here for who knows how long!"

"What?" She sounds like I've brought her back from somewhere far away.

"The mudslide. The impassable road. I hope it doesn't mess up your plans too badly."

She stares at me, uncomprehending. I smile and hold out my hand. "Greg Stern," I introduce myself.

"Priscilla," she says quietly, not looking at me and not taking my hand. Bingo.

Rakesh sits down across from me. His eyes behind his wire-rim glasses twitch more than usual. Raindrops weigh down his long eyelashes. "Hey Greg, what do you make of this? Cut off from the outside world. Can you believe this is happening in the twenty-first century in the civilized world?" he asks.

I try to signal him to shut up. I want to talk to Priscilla, but he doesn't get it.

"Does it mess up your schedule?" he asks across the table.

"I was supposed to stay here a few more days anyway," I say. "What about you?"

"I'm really good with this. I'm actually happy for a longer reprieve from going back to work. My job is so stressful; I'm grateful for every day I don't have to sit in front of my computer for thirteen hours."

"I hear you, man. But when you get back, there'll be hell to pay."

"Probably. But in the meantime—pure bliss." He stretches his legs out and pleasurably sips his coffee.

"I just wish they had some beer," I say, and turn back to Priscilla. "Are you glad to stay a little longer?"

"Yes," she whispers, avoiding eye contact.

"Not a great situation to go back to, huh?" I probe.

"No," she responds in the same expressionless, almost inaudible voice.

This wasn't exactly helpful. I've no idea how to draw her out. Maybe I'm the wrong person for this. Another woman would be better. I see fear in her eyes. But why?

9:00 A.M.

At breakfast, now reduced to hot oatmeal and dried fruit due to the food rationing, I sit next to Cora.

"I tried to talk to Priscilla today," I begin. "She seems totally traumatized."

"She's been through a rough patch," Cora confirms.

"The usual?" I ask. "Drugs and prostitution?"

Cora looks at me sharply and narrows her eyes. "Mr. Stern, what is the purpose of your curiosity? If you want sensational stories about the plight of inner-city black women, I'm sure you can find plenty of examples in the library or the newspapers."

Ouch. That stings. "I apologize, Ms. Cora. No idle curiosity, just human concern. I feel sorry for the girl and mean no offense," I say in a soothing voice, I hope.

"Men of your race, age, and social class tend to show an unsavory curiosity about the sexual misery of young black women. And by the way, my name is Mrs. Howard, not Ms. anything."

"My apologies again, Mrs. Howard. You call me by my last name and I should have called you Mrs. Howard all along."

She nods with dignity. "Priscilla," she pauses, somewhat appeased, "she went through some stuff that's a lot worse than 'the usual,' as you call it. Years of physical and emotional abuse."

I cringe. "You're right. I have no idea what Pricilla went through. There's nothing 'usual' about it. It was a cruel and thoughtless phrase. I have no right to pry. I'm sorry."

"Are you?" she asks.

Am I? Yes, I do feel sorry for Priscilla. What does she expect me to say? "Did Priscilla know Clarita before she came here?" I redirect.

"No, she just knew Clarita by reputation, from what we told her, until this retreat."

"I'm reading her book on freedom right now." Maybe this will get me some brownie points.

"Are you enjoying it?" she asks.

I better fess up. "To be honest with you, Mrs. Howard, it's not easy for me to grasp what she's saying in the book. I regret that I never met Abbess Clarita in person."

"Thank you for your honesty, Mr. Stern. There's a huge difference between reading words in a book and being in the teacher's presence. Have you heard of transmission?"

"I've heard it mentioned before, but I'm not clear on what it means." I'm hoping Cora can give me a reasonably short explanation, preferably without any riddles.

"A transmission is a kind of mind-merge, Mr. Stern."

"Like in *Star Trek*, when the Vulcans touch a human's head with their fingertips?"

"Sort of like that. Since Zen doesn't really teach anything…"

"…it only points the way," I finish the sentence.

"Do you want me to continue, Mr. Stern?" she asks.

"Sorry for interrupting. I think there's a Suzuki quote about this."

"There is, Mr. Stern. Suzuki Roshi said, 'Unless it grows out of yourself, no knowledge is really yours, it is only borrowed plumage.'"

"I actually get that. I've always resisted accepting stuff teachers told me or wrote about. I have to experience it myself."

"There you go."

"That's it?" I can't believe it's that easy.

"You pretty much got it."

"So, the teacher does a mind-merge like in *Star Trek* and then the knowledge appears in the student's mind? Like downloading data from a computer onto a flash drive?"

"No, that doesn't sound right. I'm not a Zen Master; I didn't get a direct transmission. Maybe you should talk to someone more qualified. But a mind's not a computer. A mind is organic and needs to be ready to receive the transmission after years of meditation."

"I figured it couldn't be that easy."

"It never is." She's finished her breakfast and prepares to get up from the table.

"So Priscilla spent a week here in Clarita's presence, before the abbess was murdered?"

"That she did, and I think it changed her profoundly."

"Not for the better, apparently."

"Sometimes you have to get worse before you get better," Mrs. Howard says cryptically and gets up to leave.

I stir my cold coffee and decide that I've reached my limit of Zen wisdom for the day. All these riddles make my head hurt.

11:00 A.M.

I trudge over to the bathhouse to soak in the indoor tub. It's still raining. I'm dripping wet and my flip-flops are getting stuck in the mud.

In the hot tub I find the usual suspects: Rakesh, his glasses all fogged up; Hans, his skin red like a lobster; Dylan with his wet ponytail, and Bill, the builder.

"It doesn't look good for Jacob," Rakesh observes darkly. "I've hiked a lot of these trails, and believe me, they're treacherous even without rain. In this weather, you'd be slipping and sliding like on a Mammoth Mountain ski slope."

I nod. "Plus the forest rangers and police can't even search for him right now. They're busy with the mudslide and trying to keep everybody else safe."

"And he didn't take his gear," Hans adds, smacking the water with one beefy hand.

"Well, if he was careless enough to go out on the mountain at night, he must have known the risk of an accident ending badly," Bill says.

"If it *was* an accident." Dylan seems to know something we don't.

"What else would it be?" Bill asks.

"Haven't you noticed, Bill? The body count is rising," Rakesh says.

"The police are treating this as a suspicious disappearance," says Dylan.

I shift on the submerged rocks to find a more comfortable position. "How'd you know?"

"I work in the kitchen. Abelli and his team set up their command center at a back table there. I overheard them talking."

Even in the hot water, it gives me chills to think that I'm stuck here with a double murderer in our midst.

3:00 P.M.

The office has a new manager. I recognize the Ino who assigns my seat every morning. He looks at me with cold, unblinking eyes and informs me, "We have to log every outgoing and incoming call in this book, Mr. Stern. Please note the time of your call, your name, the phone number, and the name of the party you are calling."

This is starting to feel a lot like prison. Don't I have any right to privacy?

"Are you allowed to do this?" I ask the strict-looking Ino. I already miss the gentle Jacob.

"It's voluntary, but it wouldn't look good if you refused. It's for our own protection."

"How does this protect me?"

"Do you want to refuse?"

"No," I sigh and begin dialing. "I'm only calling my wife."

"Vega," I say, once I get a connection.

"Greg, how are you holding up in the rain?"

"It's bad. We're cut off by a mudslide, the roof of my cabin leaks, and Brother Jacob has disappeared."

"Oh no, Brother Jacob is such a gentle soul. When did he disappear?"

"Two days ago. Also, they're monitoring our phone calls and rationing our food."

She chuckles. "Sorry, I know it's not funny, but you sound like a disaster victim."

"I am a disaster victim."

She ignores my comment. "Oh God, how's Jacob going to survive out there in the rain?"

"If he's even still alive."

"What are you saying?"

"He may have overheard something. Listen, I can't talk, but I want you to look into something." I turn around to see if the Ino is listening in. He's busy with a guest, who wants to buy some items from the gift shop. I snatch a fragment from their conversation: "I'm all out of fresh clothes and books to read."

It's safe to talk. "There's this weird project going on here. DB Builders are planning it," I whisper.

"I already researched it. They're a huge company building big resort developments in Hawaii and the Caribbean. I tried to find out about the project at the hot springs, but they deny any involvement at the Zen Center. It doesn't exist, according to their rep."

"But their equipment and workers are here."

"I know."

"There is something else. But I can't talk about it. Not on the telephone under the circumstances."

"Something about Clarita? Just say yes or no," Vega prompts me.

"Yes."

"Something about her past?" she asks.

"Yes."

"I heard rumors, Greg. I'm really sorry you got mixed up in all this. As soon as this mudslide has been removed I want you to come home."

"So do I. This place is like an inverted Shangri-La. It's in a remote, hidden valley, and has healing hot springs, but instead of prolonging people's lives, they get murdered."

4:00 P.M.

I leave the office and wonder where to go. The dining hall is closed and my cabin is leaking and wet. The only choices are the Zen-do—and I'm not feeling it—and the library. They also opened the yoga center for people to get out of the rain. Rakesh said they're offering free massages there for the guests to de-stress. Definitely the most attractive option. I trudge through the mud from the office along the main path toward the yoga center at the western edge of the retreat. Rain is pelting my plastic poncho. At the turn-off up the hill to the Suzuki Roshi memorial I dodge rivulets of rainwater streaming down the slope.

What a change from the pine-scented, shady mountain trail we climbed in procession just a couple of days ago. Fortunately, Clarita's funeral wasn't scheduled for today. I watch the water carve deep ruts into the hillside. Something catches my eye. Caught behind the thin trunk of a live oak a few yards up the incline, a wet piece of fabric is wedged between the ground and the tree. I pull the hood of my poncho up a bit tighter over my head. I've got to check this out. Taking a step up the muddy slope, my foot can't get traction, and I slide backwards down the hill. I try to grab hold of branches along the way, but they snap under my weight. I go down on my knees, my elbow makes contact with the mud, while my other hand reaches for a shrub. That one has thorns, but it's sturdy and I hold on. *Shit.* Scrambling back to a standing position, I flap my arms for balance like a humming-bird on a hibiscus flower. It doesn't help. I'm going down. Maybe I should've gone to the library after all. On my butt in the mud, I look up at the tree trunk, and from this angle I see a leg attached to the piece of cloth, and a foot in one sandal.

Holy cow. I have an idea whose leg this is.

4:30 P.M.

I run back to the office as fast as the slippery trail permits and burst into the crowded space. It's full of guests waiting to make phone calls.

"A body!" I shout, trying to catch my breath. "A body on the Suzuki Memorial Trail!"

That gets everybody's attention.

"What? A body? Alive? Get the detectives!" People scramble. The Ino pales, but he keeps his composure. He runs over to the kitchen where the police have their table. "Where on the trail?" he shouts as he opens the door.

"At the bottom, close to the path. Caught on a tree trunk," I call back and collapse onto one of the armchairs, forgetting that I'm covered in mud.

· · ·

7:00 P.M.

The announcement comes at dinnertime. As if anybody was hungry, and as if the food was still good.

As usual, Haku begins: "Dear *sangha*, I'm greatly saddened to report that the body of Brother Jacob has been found today. Brother Jacob was a member of our community for seven years and we all knew him as a generous and gentle man, kind and patient to everybody. A great nature lover, he was also an advanced practitioner. Jacob will join his teacher and will be buried at the memorial next to Abbess Clarita. Detective Abelli will give you the details now."

He steps back, and Abelli takes over. His appearance has steadily deteriorated these last two days. His longish hair looks greasy, and his borrowed jeans are crumpled and stained.

"I'm sorry to be the bearer of more bad news," he begins. "We have recovered Brother Jacob's body on the Suzuki Memorial Trail. Only an autopsy can establish cause and time of death. Unfortunately, we can't transport the body to the medical examiner at this time."

"There's a helicopter pad here," someone calls out.

"Is that true?" Abelli turns to Haku.

Haku grimaces. "Technically it's true, but the helipad has never been used and is overgrown with shrubs and trees. It wouldn't be safe to use it in this weather."

Abelli sighs. "Probably not. We'll order an ambulance to the other side of the mudslide tomorrow. We'll have to transport the body across the crevasse on a stretcher."

Too much information, I think.

9:30 P.M.

We are "invited" to spend the night in the yoga center if our cabins leak. Mine is completely soaked. There's no dry spot to be found even in the middle of the floor. So I pack up a blanket and a pillow from the clammy futon and shoulder my bag for the "evacuation."

In the open space of the yoga center, I bed down on the tatami mat next to Rakesh.

"So you found another body," he greets me. "Congratulations. I don't know if I want to sleep next to you, man."

"I only found him, I didn't do him in," I answer. "Besides, it could've been an accident."

"Accident, my eye," Rakesh says. "One of these people here is a killer," he adds in a mock-scary voice.

"Yeah, we should have a movie night to go with the slumber party. I suggest something by Agatha Christie—*And Then There Were None.*"

"I prefer *The Shining*," Rakesh says with a grin.

"As if things couldn't get worse, I have to put up with your taunts," I say.

"Look at the bright side, Greg. If one of us gets attacked tonight, the other can come to his aid."

"As if you know how to defend us," I tease him.

He raises his walking stick triumphantly.

3:00 A.M.

I didn't expect a good night's sleep and I don't get one.

Sometime before dawn—no clocks, remember—I wake up to moaning and screaming coming from the center of the room. Rakesh is up already.

"Someone turn on the lights," I say sleepily.

"The power's out from the storm, and the solar panels haven't been charging."

I hear soothing voices, and finally a wobbly hurricane lamp is produced and carried to the origin of the commotion.

"What the heck," Rakesh mumbles next to me.

The moaning has morphed into gasping, choking, or vomiting.

"Oh great. That's all we need, vomit all over the bamboo floor," Rakesh complains.

"I should've signed up for army boot camp instead of a Zen retreat. It would've been more relaxing," I mutter.

The flickering light partially reveals the source of the agitation: a young, black face distorted in agony. Priscilla.

"No, don't hit me! Don't hurt me!" Priscilla screams.

Rakesh and I jump up to defend her. He's armed with his walking stick and I grab an exercise weight. We rush over to Priscilla's spot. Who's attacking her?

"Calm down," Cora tells Priscilla and us. "Nobody's attacking her. She's just freaking out."

We lower our weapons. Cora and her companions rally around Priscilla, rub her back, make soothing noises, hold her hands, but she's not to be comforted.

"Don't force me! Please leave me alone!" she screams.

"Get a first aid kit and the nurse," Cora tells the Ino, who has slept in the space with the guests.

He nods and runs out into the rain.

Priscilla is convulsing and seems to be going into a seizure.

"Is there a doctor in the house?" Cora yells.

An elderly man gets up from his mat. "I'm an anesthesiologist," he says.

Perfect. Maybe he can put us all to sleep.

"No, leave me! I can't do it! Please let me go!" Priscilla screams. She's choking, coughing, vomiting.

"Who's she talking to?" I ask. Rakesh shrugs.

"Shh, girl, nobody's hurting you. You're safe, we're here," Cora tells her. "It's all over now, you're here with us. He can't hurt you anymore. It's all in the past."

Priscilla sobs. The doctor hands a pill from his bag to Cora. "Give her this—it will calm her down."

With the help of Mary on Priscilla's other side, Cora tries to administer the pill. But Priscilla is having none of it. "He's going to kill me. I can't do it," she sobs.

"No one's going to kill you, girl. We're all here protecting you. Even these fine men with their stick and gym equipment." She looks at Rakesh and me.

I hide the weight behind my back and try to slink into the background. Rakesh looks sheepish and lowers his stick.

"Don't force me to do it. I can't," Priscilla cries.

Nomi and Abelli rush into the hall. Abelli's carrying a powerful flashlight and Nomi is bringing a first aid kit. She kneels down next to Priscilla and pulls out a syringe from her kit.

"What's going on?" Abelli demands. "Is someone trying to hurt her?" He's wearing an oversized brown Zen robe someone must have lent him. He was trapped by the rain and the mudslide without luggage. This robe must hurt his sartorial pride.

"It's the trauma of her past year," Cora says. "The anxiety came back up, probably from the stress. She was severely abused."

"Why'd she say 'Don't kill me. I can't do it'? Who's she talking about?" Abelli asks.

"I've no idea. She almost died at the hands of her abuser," Cora explains.

Abelli kneels down next to Nomi and Priscilla. Nomi has drawn the syringe and is about to inject it when Priscilla has another outburst. "No, not the syringe!" She swats at Nomi.

"Priscilla," Abelli asks calmly, "what can't you do? Who's trying to force you?"

"Don't punish me! I can't do it," she pleads.

"No one's punishing you; no one's accusing you, girl," Cora assures her.

"What can't you do? Did someone send you here?" Abelli probes.

"Stop it right now!" Cora demands. "Don't you see this girl is having a breakdown? How dare you interrogate her at a time like this?"

Abelli steps back, chastised. But I know what he is thinking, because I'm thinking the same thing.

6

Day 7: 5:30 A.M.
Nobody has slept much when the bell ringer wakes us, and we are relieved that this night is over.

Priscilla's spot in the middle of the floor is empty. They must have transferred her to the main building. The rain turned to a drizzle. I'm not sure I have it in me to meditate, but it sounds appealing to sit quietly for a while in a calm and dry spot. Rakesh and I trudge to the Zen-do.

"What a night," I say.

Rakesh nods. "You can say that again. What's going on here?"

A bizarre procession is moving toward the parked monastery van. Cora supports Priscilla on one side with Abelli on the other. He's now dressed in a wrinkled, muddy suit. He carries two bags in his free hand. They must belong to the women. Dylan and the Ino follow behind, carrying a stretcher with a covered figure—Jacob. Gray drizzle sprinkles the scene.

"What a pitiful picture," Rakesh remarks.

"They must've ordered an ambulance to the other side of the mudslide."

"Lucky them. I'd like to get out in that van too," Rakesh says, watching the white monastery van longingly.

"Not unless you're either a corpse or a nutcase," I say.

"I'm not sure if Cora and Abelli are supporting Priscilla or if she's under arrest," Rakesh observes, cleaning his glasses.

"You heard her; she claims she didn't do it."

"Didn't do what?"

I shrug.

"Why's Cora get to leave?"

"Rakesh, she's taking care of Priscilla. And she's a teacher and has small kids. She's obviously a higher priority to get out of here than a techno nerd like you. Your computers won't die without you."

"That hurts, man. My computer programs are getting seriously overloaded without me."

Hans Becker joins us watching the parade. He looks the worse for wear. His blond hair is unkempt, his white T-shirt is muddy, his work pants are ripped and expose a piece of his burly calf.

"What happened to you?" Rakesh asks. "You look like hell."

"I need to get out of here," Hans says in a strange, high-pitched voice that doesn't seem to belong to a big man like him.

"We hear you, but since you're neither dead nor crazy, you'll have to wait," I tell him.

"I'm in danger. I'll be next if I don't get out." Hans glances over his shoulder with a paranoid expression, as if a group of zombies were about to materialize out of the fog any minute.

"What's the panic?" I ask. Is everybody descending into an existential crisis here?

"I have information that's probably more damaging than

Jacob's. I overheard something too. If I stay here, they'll carry me out next."

Rakesh rolls his eyes behind his wire-rim glasses.

"What'd you overhear? Damaging to whom?" I want specifics.

"I can't tell you, or else I'll put you in danger too."

Hans sounds a bit overly dramatic, but looking around at the miserable group of people in mud-stained clothes, shivering in the damp morning air, it's hard to remain optimistic. "Thanks for the consideration, but we're all stuck here in the mud."

"I need to talk to Abelli right away." Hans still has that panicked look and strained voice.

"You better hurry—he's about to get into that van," Rakesh tells him.

"I need to get into that van too."

Hans is a heavy man with big bones. Even if they agreed to take him, I don't think he would fit inside the van. Rakesh must have been thinking the same thing, because he says, "Good luck with that."

"Did you overhear something Bill said?" I ask him.

"Yes. Beware of that man." Hans is rocking back and forth as if trying to gather momentum.

"We'll take that to heart, Hans. But Greg and I travel together and we're armed." Rakesh holds up his ridiculous walking stick.

"Put it down, Rakesh. I wouldn't brag about that thing," I tell him.

"Better than nothing. Last night I saw you brandishing a gym weight."

"Touché. Guilty as charged." I grin.

"I gotta go." Becker runs up to Abelli and starts to petition him with urgency.

We watch the detective's reaction. He also looks like hell. Greasy hair, black bags under his eyes. He shakes his head wearily. Hans Becker's voice rises a notch. Abelli points to the stretcher and Priscilla, who moves like a zombie, more dragged than led between her support people on either side. Abelli sighs and motions to one of the people standing and watching. Haku is nowhere to be seen. He must be in the Zen-do meditating.

"Someone please get Officer Rodriguez. He's in one of the guest rooms behind the kitchen. He'll stay here until I get back," Abelli calls to the assembled crowd. "Mr. Becker, you can make a statement to Sergeant Rodriguez, and then stay in his presence, if you don't feel safe, until I get back."

Becker's face is tense and his hands are balled into fists.

"I don't feel safe either," one of the female guests shouts out.

"Me neither," Mary agrees.

Abelli looks at Becker. "See what you have created?"

Becker nods. His face is bright red now.

"We have to find out what Bill said," Rakesh insists.

"Where is Bill, anyway? I haven't seen him since yesterday, and he's not part of the good-bye committee for Priscilla and Cora."

Rakesh looks around. "I didn't see him at the yoga center last night. You think he stayed at his cabin?"

"Maybe. I wish I could be a fly on the wall of this ambulance. I want to hear what they say about Jacob's 'accident,' and Priscilla's confession of 'not doing it,'" I say.

"They don't allow flies in an ambulance, Greg."

The van with Abelli, Cora, Priscilla, and Jacob's body departs under the yearning glances of everybody left behind. The spectacle is over and people disperse in different directions.

I have no place to go and my curiosity is nagging at me, so I ask Rakesh, "Are you up for doing some investigating on our own?"

"Sure, Greg. We've missed meditation and breakfast is not until nine. I've got nothing better to do."

"I like your spirit, Rakesh. Let's go."

"Could I have a cup of coffee first? I'm wet and cold." Rakesh shudders to make his point.

"We have to take care of your creature comforts," I assure him as we make out way to coffee station in the dining court.

"Asshole," he says.

I grin. We're becoming really good friends.

7:30 A.M.

We hold our hot coffee mugs with both hands for a little warmth while looking at the creek below. It has swollen to the size of small river. We listen to the sound of water rushing over the boulders. I tell Rakesh I want to go back to the Suzuki Memorial Trail, where I found Jacob's body. He's skeptical. "What do you expect to find there that the police overlooked, after two days of torrential rain?"

"I realize it's a long shot, but I just want to see the site once more. Jacob wore his sandals and indoor clothing. Why would he go up there in a storm, dressed like that?"

We set off on the path.

"We've been over that," Rakesh says while dodging a huge puddle in the path. "It obviously doesn't make sense. Someone either forced him to go up there or gave him a very compelling and urgent reason to go."

Frankly, the main path hasn't improved much. With each step we have to extract our feet from the mud with a sucking sound. I agree with Rakesh that all arguments speak against an accident. Now we just have to figure out why Jacob went on the trail, who or what compelled him to go there in the middle of a storm.

"We have to find some clues," I say to Rakesh.

"All the clues have long been washed away."

He has a good point there. We stumble along. The rain has almost stopped, but the world around us looks gray and colorless.

"Rakesh, you knew Jacob a little better than I did. What would have compelled him to drop everything and run up to the memorial?" I finally ask.

Rakesh comes up with an answer right away: "An emergency. Someone in trouble. He would've dropped everything to help.

"The emergency could have been called in by phone, and Jacob was the first person to answer any call. Or a guest could have appealed to him for help, most likely about someone wounded or hurt."

I place my feet carefully, trying not to fall and hurt myself. Nomi is the registered nurse on the staff, so Jacob would have turned to her and her first aid kit in case of a medical crisis. Since nobody has a cell phone here, it could have been difficult to locate Nomi in the darkness and the storm.

"If he couldn't find Nomi, Jacob would've grabbed the Red Cross kit from the office and gone himself," Rakesh concludes.

"Agreed." I stop and catch my breath. The air feels fresh and cool in my lungs after the rain.

We have reached the turn-off to the memorial, the spot where I found Jacob's dead body. I show Rakesh the skinny little oak tree, where the body was wedged behind the trunk. Rakesh imagines that someone met Jacob at the memorial, whacked him, and pushed him down the hill. But I'm not so sure.

"That's one of my questions: Was Jacob pushed down the hill, or was he intercepted on his way up? Was there a struggle?"

We start climbing up the hill, but we are not getting very far. The hillside is too slippery, as it was on the night of the murder. It's too steep. The killer must have waited for Jacob just about here. Pulled him off the trail, hit him, pushed him down, or just let him slump down. It was dark by then and nobody would have heard anything. Rakesh thinks the killer had an accomplice. A person to call in an emergency.

I disagree. "What if someone, let's say, Bill the Builder, ran into the office and alarmed Jacob that a guest fell and got hurt on the Memorial Trail? Jacob has to come immediately. No time for rain gear. Just grab the first aid kit and rush back together. They go a few steps up the trail, Bill whacks him with a stone or one of his tools, Jacob slides down the hill, and Bill walks away."

"Pretty risky," Rakesh says. "Someone could have seen him so close to the path."

"It was the night of the major rainstorm. Nobody was out, and visibility was close to zero."

"Was there a struggle? What were Jacob's injuries?" Rakesh is trying to reconstruct the encounter in his mind.

"I only remember a bloody wound on his forehead, but I couldn't tell if it was from a blow or from the fall."

"Now all we need is evidence that Bill was here and hit Jacob with intent to kill."

"I love your optimism, Rakesh." We are perched on the slick trail, holding onto bushes and tree trunks to keep from sliding down. Not a great position for a careful reconstruction of events.

"Ouch, these shrubs have thorns," Rakesh cries. As he grabs one of the branches for stability, I notice a tiny red dot. A small spot of color in a gray landscape.

"Look at this piece of fabric skewered on a thorn," I point out. "It looks like a piece of Bill's favorite maroon polo shirt."

"It's evidence! Let's take it!" Rakesh is excited.

"It's not evidence anymore once we remove it. We have to get Rodriguez over here and the police have to match the fabric."

"It's something. It proves Bill was here."

"It only proves his shirt was here."

Rakesh ignores me. He has this all figured out in his mind. "I bet Bill lured Jacob to the trail and hit him over the head."

"But why?"

"Isn't it obvious? Because Jacob overheard him fighting with Dick Baxter on the phone. Baxter accused Bill of the murder. Bill threatened Hans not to say anything. That's enough reason to whack Jacob over the head."

"I don't know. Let's go before we slide down the hill."

Rakesh lets go of the shrub and promptly falls on his butt.

8:30 A.M.

We find Officer Rodriguez in the back of the kitchen at a table with Hans Becker, who's signing a statement. The kitchen crew is getting ready for breakfast. It looks like leftovers, but at least there's fresh-baked bread. My stomach is growling

Rodriguez shakes Hans's hand and says, "Thank you for your testimony, Mr. Becker. Stick around, people. Don't wander off by yourself."

Hans swallows. He's white as a sheet and looks positively terrified. He moves toward the dining hall with small hesitant steps, glancing back over his shoulder at us.

We take Rodriguez to the trail to show him the evidence. He takes photographs, puts more yellow crime-scene tape around the site, and bags the piece of fabric.

By the time we get back, breakfast is over. We find some bread, butter, and jam and sit at the table with Hans.

"Okay, Hans, we'll tell you what we found, if you tell us what you overheard," I prompt him.

We chew our bread and Hans begins. "First you should know that we're not here at the Zen Center's invitation. What we're doing here is more like a hostile takeover. The monastery is deep in debt and DB Builders wants to buy the land cheaply to create a health spa resort at the hot springs."

We nod. "We figured as much."

"Abbess Clarita was dead set against the plan," Hans continues.

"She would be," Rakesh says.

"So we're doing this survey knowing we're not wanted."

"Get to the point, Hans. What did you overhear?"

"'What else do you want me to do? Haven't I done enough?'"

"What?" I ask, confused.

"That's what I overheard," Hans says. "Bill shouted it when he talked to Dick Baxter on the phone. I was in the office, and so was Jacob. Bill really lost it."

"Hmm, that could be interpreted in different ways. Like, 'What else do you want me to do besides the survey?'" It doesn't sound too ominous to me.

"You don't know the context. Bill wanted to get out of here; Dick wanted to close the deal."

Hans's voice is shaky and he keeps kneading a piece of bread in his hand and nervously wringing his napkin, but I can't quite see the threat. "Okay, still not conclusive," I tell him.

"Don't you see? Dick thought Bill messed up. With the murder investigation going on, Baxter couldn't buy the property. It's all tied up legally."

I don't see and neither does Rakesh. "That's what you're so afraid of?" he asks.

"Wouldn't you be?" Hans is sweating and his voice rises a pitch.

I don't want him to get all worked up, so I admit that the evidence points to Bill, but Bill hasn't really gained anything.

"That's what Baxter said. He yelled at Bill for screwing up, implicating DB in murder, with the orange rope and all. When we were outside the office, Bill turned to me and said,

'You better not repeat anything you heard in there, if you want to keep your job.'"

"Losing your job is a hell of a lot different than losing your life, Hans," I say.

"You guys don't get it. Jacob is dead and I'm next."

I don't know who's next. I hope nobody. Two dead bodies are enough, but the pressure must have gotten to Hans and he is in full panic mode.

We're the last ones in the dining hall, draining the final drops of coffee and chewing on the last pieces of bread.

"Where's Bill, anyway?" Rakesh asks.

As if on cue, he walks in wearing a blue polo shirt, left arm in a sling. Bill's jeans are caked with mud, he has black circles under his eyes, dirt streaks his cheek, and he has a scratch on his forehead. He looks like he's been through the ringer. But don't we all?

"Bill, where the hell have you been? What happened to you?" I ask.

"I hurt myself. I just got my wrist bandaged by the nurse." Bill grimaces and holds up his left arm. He sounds surprisingly composed, considering his appearance.

"Where'd you fall?" Rakesh asks.

"On the steep slope behind the construction site. It was super slippery. I tore up my clothes and slid down the hill. It was awful."

"By the Memorial Trail?" I ask.

"No, what would I be doing there?"

Rakesh and I look at each other. He's lying. We know he was at the Memorial Trail. Which other guest could have torn a maroon polo shirt right at that location?

"What were you doing on the slope?" Rakesh asks.

"Taking a soil sample. After the rain." Bill is all matter-of-fact, just business as usual. But is he?

Hans looks like a ghost. His eyes almost pop out of their sockets.

"No more food?" Bill checks the empty breadbaskets and tries to squeeze a drop of coffee out of the thermos dispensers.

"These are times of food rationing." Rakesh shrugs.

"Where'd you sleep last night?" I ask.

"In my cabin. It leaks, but I put up plastic sheeting from our supplies. I can't sleep in a warehouse with all those people."

"You missed all the excitement," I say.

10:30 A.M.

"I don't know about you guys, but I need a shower and a long soaking in the hot tub," I say and get up from the table. Nods all around as we gather our stuff and head over to the bathhouse.

The rain has stopped, so we sit in the steaming outdoor tub. I feel warm and relaxed watching the vapor rise into the cypress trees overhead. I am mulling things over in my mind, when Dylan joins us.

"Done with breakfast cleanup?" Rakesh asks.

"Yep," Dylan answers as he slips into the hot water.

"Did you overhear any conversations between Priscilla and Abelli?" I ask.

"When I got there this morning I saw them sitting in the back of the kitchen, but Priscilla was totally out of it. I think Nomi pumped her full of tranquilizers. She kept saying 'don't take me back there, he's going to kill me.' Abelli asked her who's going to kill her, and Cora told him to leave the girl alone."

"Yeah, we got that last night."

Dylan looks around. "But I heard this guy giving his statement to Rodriguez." He points his chin at Hans. Bill looks at Hans. Hans pales. *Oops.*

~

Nobody's making a move. We're sitting in the tub, in uncomfortable silence, when Rodriguez shows up, in full uniform. He stands at the rim of the hot tub, clears his throat, and announces, "Mr. Mason, I have to ask you to come with me for questioning."

"Now?" Bill asks.

"Now," Rodriguez confirms.

Bill has to get out of the tub in his birthday suit and follow Rodriguez into the dressing area.

Rakesh, Dylan, and I chuckle.

"Looks like you're safe for a little while," I tell Hans, who scowls at me.

2:00 P.M.

I'm so confused. I have no idea how all these pieces fit together. I decide to go to the Zen-do and sit for a while. Maybe that will clear my mind. I need a little time by myself. The meditation hall is half empty at this time of day. Sitting on my cushion, staring at the wall, I turn things over in my head. It's a muddle. Maybe if I just let go for a while and not try to think so hard, the fog will clear.

I take a few deep breaths and then, uninvited, it comes again. That feeling of being right here in my body; feeling my bare feet, my legs, my spine, my hands in my lap, my breath going in and out of my nostrils. At the same time I smell the musty mats on the platform, hear the breath of the other students, stifled noises outside, a few timid birdcalls—where have the birds been during the rain?

I don't actually have a feeling, just an awareness of myself in connection with everything around me. It's crystal clear. I'm the observer of my thoughts, and I'm also the thinker. I'm totally engaged, and simultaneously completely still and receptive. It's the sweet spot, where I'm in the moment, instead of rushing through it onto the next thought, the next sensation.

I try not to get too excited nor think too much about it, because I know, then it will evaporate. I just flow with it, one breath at a time, as if it were a stream carrying me. I'm in the right place, exactly where I need to be. Actually, there is no "I," because I've melted into the stream, I'm part of it.

Time doesn't stand still. I know the bell will ring eventually, probably sooner than I expect, but I don't feel time passing, because I move with it. I don't struggle against it, don't try to beat time, don't think about the next thing on my schedule. I'm in it. Time flies when you're having fun, they say. I say, time flows when you're in the stream. It's so nice, I could stay here forever.

The bell rings. Great, of course just when I was getting into it, it's over. Now I understand these monastics, who want to meditate for days, weeks, months on end. They just want to wallow in the pleasant stream, those greedy wise guys.

I bow and turn to my seat neighbor, smiling pleasantly. Did he experience the same thing? Probably I'm not the only Chosen One. Still, I feel pretty good about myself. Outside I get my shoes, quite excited about my insights, buoyed, lighter than I usually feel. I have to tell someone about my breakthrough.

I rush down the hill from the Zen-do to the courtyard and promptly slip on the mud. Going down, I hold out my hand to break the fall. A sharp pain shoots through my wrist up my arm. My elbow buckles as I slide down the hill, covering myself in mud.

"Cockiness comes before the fall" is probably another one of those Suzuki sayings.

～

3:00 P.M.

I shuffle through the office to the sick room in the back, cradling my hurting arm. The Ino tells me to sit down on the plastic stool while he gets the nurse. A few minutes later Nomi comes in. I wonder if it is going to work for or against me that I look pitiful and muddy.

"What are you doing here, Greg?" She stands in front of me and studies me with a skeptical expression. There's no smile on her face and no dimple in her cheek. I've tried to avoid this encounter, but now that it happened, I'll make the best of it.

"Nomi, I broke my arm just so I could see you."

Maybe her expression softens a bit, but that could be just my imagination. "I'm sorry if I offended you. I didn't mean to," I go on. "I'm an idiot sometimes, but I really respect you and what you do." Here I am again, apologizing, even though I meant no harm.

"Hmm, let me see your arm." She shifts her gaze from my face to my elbow, and moves my forearm back and forth. It hurts, but I try to stifle my complaints. To distract myself from the pain, I look around. The room lacks the simplicity and esthetic of the Zen-do and the other public spaces. It's packed with supplies, and on a narrow table papers and folders are piled up. A pillow and a blanket are bunched up at the foot of the sofa. The police use this space as their office—and apparently also as a bedroom.

"You're a trained nurse practitioner?" I ask.

"Yep, that's what I was in my former life. I don't think your arm is broken. Just a slight sprain. I'll bandage it and put it in a sling. You'll be good as new in a day or two."

With a gentle touch, she cleans my arm and puts a salve on it. I'm grateful and tell her so. After she's wrapped my arm in white bandage, I make no move to get off the sofa and out of this room. We're not done here. Nomi takes a deep breath, realizing I'm not about to leave.

"Look, Greg, I'm sorry if I have hurt your feelings, but I must be careful not to get too close to the guests, and not to let them get too close to me." She sits down on the round examination stool.

"I understand, Nomi, and I respect that. You showed me a lot, and I think you are a very brave and wise person." I pause. "Were you really afraid of getting too close to me?" That puts another spin on the situation.

"I don't want to create expectations I can't fulfill." She steps back from the sofa where I am sitting, putting the table between us.

"No expectations. You taught me that. I couldn't do what you're doing. Giving up everything and devoting your life to meditation."

"You don't need to. Your life is not a mess."

I shift on the old, worn sofa. She's right. I have it pretty good. "I just want to talk to you, Nomi. Nothing physical. Just a mind-merge."

"A mind-merge?" Nomi crinkles her brows.

"Like in *Star Trek*. Cora explained it to me. The teacher transmits the knowledge directly into the mind of the student."

"You mean a transmission?"

"Yeah, transmission. Listen, I've made progress. I just had another great meditation experience I'd like to tell you about." I have to tell someone what just happened to me in the Zen-do.

"You don't go around broadcasting your meditation experiences. They're private."

"I'm not boasting about it; I just want to tell you. You can help me accelerate the process."

"That's not how it works. If you made any progress, then you should know it can't be sped up. Time is not an issue. We don't manage or measure time."

"I got that, Nomi, I really did." I want to tell her about floating in the stream of time, but she interrupts me.

"I'm not qualified to give transmission, and you're not a student. Osho Haku is the only one here who can pass on transmission. He hasn't done it for me or any other student. We're not ready."

"You need ten thousand meditation hours, right?"

"Yep, and I still have a long way to go. Look, Greg, it's pretty busy right now; a lot of people are sick or injured. I gotta go." She looks exhausted. Her eyes have dark circles around them. I wonder how much sleep she is getting. And here I am prattling on about myself.

"I'm glad we had this talk. It was worth spraining my elbow for."

She shakes her head, smiling. At least she's not mad at me and I can still make her smile.

4:00 P.M.

With my clean bandage and muddy clothes, I go to the courtyard for a cup of tea. Rakesh and Mary are sitting on a bench, overlooking the swollen creek, heads together, giggling.

I walk over to them, teacup in the hand of my uninjured arm, holding up the other arm with the white bandages for a little sympathy.

"Hi, guys, what's going on?" I ask in my most jovial voice.

Rakesh looks up. "Nothing," he says and signals me with his eyes and eyebrows to shut up and disappear.

I pointedly ignore him. "How are things?" I ask again, expecting them to comment on my injury.

Mary is really quite good-looking. Smooth chocolate skin, large almond eyes, hair cropped close to the scalp showing off her sharply sculpted Nefertiti face, which now breaks into a smile revealing sparkling white teeth. I wonder what she sees in Rakesh with his twitching eye and wire-rim glasses. Of course he's totally smitten. But the way she looks at him, I see real emotion in her dark, expressive eyes.

"What happened to your hand?" she finally asks.

"I fell down the hill after..."

"Well, you better take care of that," Rakesh interrupts me rudely. "Mary and I were just leaving."

"Going where?" I ask, playing dumb. I know he just wants to be alone with her. Not that I blame him.

"Mary, I want to show you something," he says and takes her arm.

I wonder what he's going to "show" her. His walking stick? Well, good for him. I guess now that Cora, I mean Mrs. Howard, and Priscilla are gone, and since the other two women of Clarita's *sangha* are elderly, Mary is left behind and needs protection from the murderer on the loose.

I sit on the bench they just vacated and watch them go.

If that's how they want to play it, fine with me. I don't need their company.

I'm *so* one with the universe.

5:00 P.M.

In my cabin the tatami mats are slowly drying; it's still a bit damp, but at least it's private. I think about Vega. Would she approve of my progress? Does she wonder how I'm doing, trapped in this valley? Have I been punished enough? Did I handle the conversation with Nomi correctly? I really like her, as a person; I just don't know how to show it properly. I don't understand what women want; what do they expect from me? I'm trying to be sensitive, but somehow, it always leads to misunderstandings. Women's emotions are so complicated. Guys are much simpler.

If I could only go back to work. Running my security company based on need and demand is much more logical than cryptic Suzuki sayings and incomprehensible female emotions.

Exhausted, I take a nap. I wake up to clear skies a couple of hours later. Outside, water drops sparkle on dark green leaves in the sunshine. The trees seem to stretch luxuriously after the moisture and present themselves shiny clean. The air smells fresh. It's a whole new forest out there. I hold my face up to the warmth of the evening sun. I have a feeling things are going to turn around.

7:00 p.m.

The announcement comes at dinnertime. Abelli has undergone a transformation. He now wears well-cut black jeans, a black jean jacket, and a blue button-down shirt without tie. Still stylish, but adjusted to the circumstances. Haku is nowhere to be seen, but Abelli brought his own little bell to get our attention.

"Ladies and gentlemen, we made it over the mudslide, but I have to tell you, it was harrowing. We had to use ropes and pulleys to transport the stretcher over the slide.

"I realize you want to get out of here, but the climb over the mudslide is extremely dangerous. The rangers are working on fixing the road, but we have to ask you for a little more patience."

Moans and expressions of frustration from the crowd.

Someone must have brought a change of clothes for Abelli in the ambulance. This is completely irrelevant, but I'm fascinated by that thought.

"We have to wait for the autopsy, but we are treating Jacob's death as suspicious." He pauses and lowers his voice. "We don't want you to be alarmed."

"Really?" someone shouts. "How're we to avoid that?"

"You're safe in this controlled environment."

"It's not a controlled environment, it's a trap," Mary calls out.

"I'm here, and we have two police officers patrolling the compound. Stay in pairs or larger groups. Don't walk alone."

"Do you have any suspects?" Rakesh asks.

"We do have several strong leads, and we are following up on them. Please stay calm and enjoy your dinner." He bows out and leaves the dining hall.

Right. Enjoy the less-than-simple dinner of salad, soup, and some kind of cooked grains. The kitchen must be running out of supplies.

Dylan comes by our table and whispers, "They've been holding Bill the Builder in the exam room. For interrogation or…"

"…arrest," Hans finishes the sentence.

Dinner passes in tense silence.

We linger over dessert of yogurt and forest berries. I'd prefer a drink, or at least a glass of wine. As I'm contemplating a nice pinot noir, who walks in, making a grand entrance?

Bill the Builder in all his glory. Actually, he looks a bit ragged around the edges after hours of interrogation. Hans Becker almost faints when he sees him and seems to crawl into the seat cushion.

"Ah, there you all are," Bill says cheerfully and pulls up a chair.

Nobody answers. Bill looks around. "You thought they arrested me, didn't you? You all thought I did it, that I killed Jacob and the abbess? Well, you're wrong."

"So you convinced Abelli that the evidence lied?" I challenge him.

"Exactly. I know you tried to nail me with that piece of fabric you found at Jacob's crime scene. But I threw out that polo shirt long before Jacob died. Whoever put that scrap of fabric there, it wasn't me."

"You could prove that to the police?" I ask. Hans looks like he's seen a ghost.

"I didn't have to. I have an alibi for the night Jacob died." Bill looks around triumphantly.

"An alibi?" Rakesh asks. "Where could you have been after eight P.M. except in your cabin?"

Bill grins. He's enjoying this showdown. "I was in a meeting with Haku and the monastery's treasurer. It was a very unpleasant meeting, about the future of this place, which is in deep debt, as you may know, but neither Haku nor the treasurer can deny I was there."

Hans shakes his head in desperation.

"Is Haku in favor of building the resort?"

"No," Bill says. "The negotiations were unsuccessful."

A sigh of relief from Rakesh and Mary. Should I ask him about the abbess and the Buddha, or would that be pushing him a bit too far? Maybe a little caution might be wise. I'm caught here with no place to go.

"Well, gentlemen, lady, I'm sorry to spoil your evening, but I'm going to search around for some food. I haven't eaten since morning." He gets up and leaves us behind dumbfounded.

"How could the police let him go?" Hans hisses. "How can they believe he's innocent?"

"He's enjoying this a bit too much," I admit. There are still a lot of open questions. "I'm going to turn in. I'm exhausted." I get up to leave, when Abelli walks in.

"Could I have a word, Mr. Stern?" he asks politely.

When a police detective asks you to have a word, it's usually more than one, and it's usually not a question either. I don't have a choice.

9:00 P.M.

It's the first time we sit face to face. So far, I've only given my statements to uniformed policemen. We're in the sick room, which has been appropriated as his office.

"Please have a seat, Mr. Stern," Abelli says with a charming smile.

I sit down on the little stool Nomi used to examine my arm this morning.

"I'm glad we are finally meeting personally," he begins. "With your background in law enforcement and private security, you're familiar with problem-solving strategies, and I value your opinion."

Nice tactic. He's putting us on equal footing and assures my cooperation by appealing to my vanity. As if he were interested in my "opinion." He's putting me at ease so I'll open up. Of course, I would have done the same myself.

"Thank you for your confidence in me," I answer.

"In your work, I'm sure you share my skepticism of too many coincidences."

After buttering me up, here comes the hammer. I know what's coming next.

"You found the missing Buddha, you found Brother Jacob's body, and you found evidence at the crime scene possibly linking it to another guest."

"Were you able to link the evidence to a specific guest?" I ask, even though I know the answer from Bill.

"Ah." Abelli smiles, acknowledging my evasive maneuver. He's not going to give me any real information. "That's a good question. Whom does the evidence point to? And how did it get to the site?" He pauses for effect. A bit too dramatic for my taste.

The thought pops up in my mind that Zen doesn't teach, it only points the way, but that's irrelevant here.

"So, am I correct in assuming that you weren't able to match the piece of fabric we found with a specific person?"

"The fabric belonged to a specific person, and we both know who we are talking about. But this fact doesn't necessarily implicate the person in the murder nor provide proof that he was at the crime scene during the time in question."

I knew this already. "It could've torn off by accident; it could have been planted," I confirm.

"Where were you three nights ago between five and nine o'clock?"

"I was at dinner from seven to eight, and then I was in my cabin. If there had been any other place to go, I would've been there. But as it is, I don't have as good an alibi as Bill Mason."

"We found skin and blood samples at the site where Brother Jacob's body was found. Might we be able to trace them back to you, Mr. Stern?"

"We tore the palms of our hands holding onto the thorny branches."

"Just to be on the safe side, I'd like to ask you for a DNA sample."

"Of course."

He smiles and lets the silence hang between us. "A lot of coincidences," he finally says.

We stare at each other without a word. I can play this game too. Who blinks first? Who speaks first? Who can't stand the silence any longer? It doesn't bother me.

"I know what you're doing, Detective. I don't blame you. I'd do the same. I found the Buddha, I found the body, and I found the evidence. You figure, chances are I put them there."

"I didn't say that," he says, but he implied it and he thinks he won.

"Well, I didn't. And there's no way in hell you can prove I had anything to do with these crimes."

"Sometimes, circumstantial evidence adds up."

This guy's good. All charm and nice manners, but then bam, he snaps the whip. Now it's my turn to get some information out of him.

"What did the autopsy reveal?" I have to ask. I want to confirm what Dylan told us in the hot tub.

"An interesting point. According to the autopsy the abbess died of a heart attack, no doubt caused by the shock of the intrusion, the theft of the Buddha, and the attempted strangulation. The murderer didn't have to be particularly brutal. His mere appearance was enough."

"Hypothetically, what would be the motive?" I ask.

"Another interesting question. It seems nobody has anything to gain from Abbess Clarita's murder, the theft of the Buddha, or Brother Jacob's death."

"DB Builders profited from getting Clarita out of the way. They want to take over this property. I'm sure you talked to Dick Baxter, the company's owner."

"We did, Mr. Stern. It turns out that DB Builders doesn't benefit from the abbess's death. On the contrary. The implication of DG Builders as persons of interest in a murder case has made it impossible for them to buy the retreat. If a criminal case is pending, a sale cannot proceed. The legal obstacles are insurmountable. Their chances to take over the property were better before Clarita's death, even though she was opposed to it."

"What about Priscilla and her connection to LA gang members?"

"Yes, Priscilla is also a person of interest. There is not enough evidence to elevate her status to suspect."

"That leaves me. Am I a person of interest, or a suspect, Detective Abelli?"

"If you were a suspect, I would arrest you."

"Fortunately that's not necessary, since I have nowhere to go."

Abelli doesn't answer. He doesn't have to.

∾

10:00 P.M.

I walk out of the interview with the distinction of being in the upper echelons of the police's suspect list. I wish I had somewhere else to go besides my cabin, for a beer and some company. But there are no other options; I just have to sit by myself without any distraction. It's too dark to read, so I look at the illustrations in my cookbook and imagine Vega's reaction if I made her scalloped potatoes with smoked cheese.

A knock on the door pulls me out of my self-pity. The door is not made of solid wood, far from it. It's just a flimsy frame with a screen. It doesn't have a lock. Whoever wants to get in can. So the knock is mainly symbolic.

"Who is it?" I call.

"Greg, it's me, Hans. Can I come in?

"Go right ahead. It's open."

He steps into the room with a pillow and a sleeping bag under his arm.

"Can I please bunk here tonight?" he asks in a timid voice. Since Hans is a big, blond construction worker of German origin, I find this plea ridiculous.

"Are you serious?" I ask.

"I don't feel safe, Greg. Bill's out there. I can't believe the police let him go."

"I guess he's off their suspect list."

"How can they let me down like this, after I gave my testimony? They must know he's after me."

"Apparently they don't share your concern."

"Please, just for tonight?"

"Abelli thinks I'm a suspect. You should be afraid of me."

"I know you didn't do it."

"How can you be so sure?"

"I trust you."

"Why don't you bunk with Rakesh?"

"I tried, but he's not alone." He gives me a meaningful wink.

"I see. Okay, I guess you can sleep over there on Vega's futon. But don't bother me." I turn to the wall and close my eyes.

"Thanks, Greg."

Despite my warning, uninterrupted sleep is not to be for the second night in a row. In the early morning hours, someone is shaking me roughly.

"Wake up, Greg."

"What? I told you not to bother me."

"I hear noises outside."

"Stop shaking me. I don't hear anything. Go back to sleep."

"Do you have a weapon?" he asks.

"A switchblade knife," I mumble.

"Where is it?"

"In one of these drawers." I'm not opening my eyes. "Hans, don't pull a Priscilla on me. I'm tired."

"I'm having an existential crisis, Greg."

"Why don't you take yourself and your existential crisis out of my cabin right now?"

"I can't go out there. Don't you hear the noise?"

"I don't hear anything, but I'll go out there and check if you promise to leave me the hell alone for the rest of the night."

"I promise."

Cursing and mumbling to myself, I get up and stagger to the door.

I open the door and step outside into the clear, crisp night. I take in a lungful of fresh oxygen and look up at the black sky sparkling with millions of brilliant stars. In the distance I hear the gurgling stream. That's absolutely all I hear.

"All clear out there; a peaceful night," I report back to Hans, who sits on his futon, sleeping bag drawn up all the way to his chin. "I don't want to hear another peep out of you for the rest of the night."

7

D ay 8: 5:30 A.M.
　　　I get up with the wake-up bell and leave Hans behind. He's dead to the world, snoring on Vega's futon. I'm not going to take him in ever again. Once was enough.

At meditation, all I can think about are the allegations against me in this convoluted case. If Bill didn't do it (and this is still a big IF in my mind), and if Priscilla didn't do it (I'm still doubtful about that as well), and if I didn't do it (at least I'm certain about that), then who did it? There is only one other person I can think of, who benefited two ways from Clarita's death: Osho Haku. First, he got the abbot's job, and I have a feeling he likes the power. Secondly, he thwarted the hated takeover by DB Builders, because they are now tied up in the investigation.

Time to talk to the Zen Master.

7:00 a.m.
　　　It's pretty difficult to get an appointment with the Osho. I have to throw my weight around with the Ino, and pressure

him by pointing out the hardship this whole ordeal presents to my wife and me. Vega has been a friend and supporter of the monastery for years, so finally, he grants me fifteen minutes before breakfast. I take it.

The Ino leads me to a small Spartan room off the Zen-do. The abbot's office. There are no chairs, no desk. We sit on cushions. I guess that helps to keep the meetings short.

"Mr. Stern," Haku says. "The Ino tells me you have an urgent concern you need to discuss with me. How can I help you?"

No "good morning," no small talk. He's all business, sitting cross-legged and ramrod straight behind a low table that must serve as his desk.

"Thank you for seeing me," I acknowledge, as I clumsily get down on the pillow facing him.

"It's highly irregular," he says. "I'm extremely busy with the responsibility for all the people detained here and two murder cases."

"I can imagine."

"Can you?" he asks in a terse tone. "If that's the case, then please come straight to the point and tell me what's so important you couldn't discuss it with the police or any other staff member."

This is not going to be easy. He's not like Abelli or anybody else I know. I have no idea how he ticks.

"As you know," I begin, trying hard not to waste time, "I found the missing Buddha, I found Brother Jacob's body, and I found evidence. Consequently, the police consider me a suspect."

"As they should," he says coldly.

"I wanted to appeal to you."

"Appeal for what?"

"You are a spiritual authority. You must be a great judge of character. I want to appeal to you to vouch for my sincerity and innocence."

He looks at me. "You're kidding, right?"

"Receiving transmission and thousands of hours of meditation must change a man," I insist.

"Not to the point where I can read a person's mind and soul."

"But you must have deep insights. I can't even imagine sitting all these hours, years..."

"It flew by."

I laugh at the joke. Look at him sitting across from me stone-faced. He's not joking.

"If someone kills another person, doesn't that create terrible karma?" I ask.

"Irreversible," he states. "Look, Mr. Stern, if you are interested in the fundamentals of Zen Buddhism, I suggest you seek out our bookstore or library and read Suzuki Roshi's *Zen Mind — Beginner's Mind*, but I don't have time for this. If you'll excuse me, I have a monastery to run." He gets up fluidly from his cushion, and I scramble up from mine.

"Thank you for your time," I say and hold out my hand.

He ignores it, narrows his eyes, and hits me with a glacial cold front of contempt. I've never felt anything like it. I guess that's what ten thousand hours of meditation can do.

10:30 A.M.

After breakfast, I find Nomi in the garden next to my cabin, pulling weeds. This time, I don't ask, I just kneel down beside her and help. The weeds are tall, but they come out easily after the rain.

"How's the elbow?" she asks, without looking up.

"Good as new. It was nothing serious, as you said. I took the bandage off."

"You should keep it on a little longer. I'll give you an elbow brace in a day or two."

"I spoke to Haku."

"How'd that go?"

"Not very well."

She laughs. "I'm surprised he even talked to you."

"I had to push for it."

"Why?"

"I had some questions only he could answer."

"Did he?"

"No. He referred me to the library and some Suzuki book about Beginner's Mind."

Nomi laughs again. "That sounds about right."

"I'm too insignificant to talk to him."

"Yes, you are. But you're in good company. Most of us are too insignificant, including me."

"Isn't that pretty arrogant?"

"Greg, a Zen monastery is no democracy. We're not all equal. Not at all. There's quite a hierarchy."

"That doesn't sound very Buddhist to me."

"What's your definition of 'Buddhist'? Where do you get your insights about Buddhism?"

"Alright, alright. Mostly I get my ideas about Buddhism from you." At least we're talking; I'm happy about that. "So you agree that I'm not ready to talk to Haku?"

"You're not."

"Why not? And how does he know?"

"Greg," she laughs, "it's not hard to notice."

"Is it my attitude? Can he look into my heart?"

"If it weren't a cliché, I'd say you wear your heart on your sleeve. You're not very hard to read."

"I'm not humble enough, right?"

"For starters."

"Look at me: I'm on my knees pulling weeds from the mud. How much more humble can I get?"

To demonstrate my point, I pull a huge dandelion with its roots out of the ground and place it on the pile of weeds beside us.

"I appreciate your help, but I bet in five minutes maximum you'll have had enough."

"Nomi, Nomi, you know me too well." I might as well sit down on the garden bench.

"Like I said, it's not that difficult." Nomi remains on her knees in front of the flower bed.

"All these hours of meditation have made you too wise."

This makes her smile, and I get to see her dimples. "What did you and Haku talk about?"

"Karma. Like, when you kill someone."

"Unforgivable." She pushes a strand of hair out of her face and sits next to me.

"That's what he said."

"Of course. Don't you have the same in Christianity? A mortal sin?"

"Yeah, but you can go to confession." Not that I've ever been.

"You still think Haku had something to do with Clarita's death?"

"I don't know what to think anymore. The police consider me a suspect. At least I know I didn't do it."

"It will reveal itself," she says.

"You mean, the killer will reveal himself voluntarily? I don't think so."

"Not he, but whatever caused these events, will reveal itself."

"You really think so?"

"Absolutely."

The skeptic in my mind comes up with the argument that big revelations need a little help from old-fashioned investigation, but I keep that thought to myself. "What if we never find out what happened?"

"What happened, how it happened, why it happened, and what it set into motion is all part of the flow of life. The great lesson is to observe life revealing and manifesting itself."

"Nomi, you're talking in riddles again."

She laughs. "Never mind. All I'm trying to say is, don't worry so much."

"I can't just sit and watch," I protest.

"Why not?"

"We have to take responsibility in what happens, take control. To make things better, or at least prevent them from getting worse." I'm just stating the obvious here.

She looks at me strangely, with a little smile. "Do you really understand all the consequences of your actions, when you try to make things better?"

"We can never predict all the consequences of our actions to the nth degree. But at least we can try."

"Most interventions, even well-meaning ones, lead to desastrous results. Look at the consequences of logging, destroying whole eco systems and causing erosion. That's why we live here in a remote monastery, Greg. We try not to manipulate life. We just let it unfold in us and through us."

"What does that mean? Do you believe in predetermination? Is everything just fate and you have no free will to change it?"

"Of course you have free will. Every moment you can either accept life or reject it. Life is our only teacher. You can embrace the flow or struggle against it."

"Nomi, you're giving me a headache."

"Yeah, headaches usually come from struggling against life."

"Do you have an aspirin?"

She laughs and hands me a couple of pills from her pocket.

9:00 P.M.

I'm lying on my futon, staring into space. The solar-powered overhead light is too dim to read and there are no outlets to plug in anything stronger. The illustrations in the *Zen Cookbook* only make me hungry. In my mind, I replay the conversation with Haku, trying to read between the lines. What did Haku reveal about himself? He stonewalled me, demonstrating his arrogance and superiority; he obviously loves to have power over others and enjoys putting them in their place. I doubt Abbess Clarita would have acted this way. But what does this behavior point to? It means he's either really too busy to listen to me or feeling guilty.

My musings are interrupted by a knock on my door.

"Hans, go away. You can't sleep here again. You snore and I'm tired of being woken up in the middle of the night."

Pause.

"Ahem, it's me, Nomi."

I jump up from my bed and rush to the door.

"Nomi, what're you doing here?" I ask, standing in the doorway.

"Can I come in?" she asks in a timid little voice.

"Yeah, sure." I step aside. "Sorry there's no chair. You have to sit on the ground or on the futon."

"I know. I clean these cabins." She sits down cross-legged in one fluid motion.

"Of course you know," I acknowledge. My voice sounds a bit nervous. "What brings you here?"

She holds up a thick, rolled cigarette. Well, it's a joint.

"You want to smoke this here? I don't think smoking is allowed in the cabins." I sound pretty uncertain.

"If you won't say anything, I won't say anything."

"Okay, there's also the fire danger…"

"After the torrential downpour?"

"Good point," I admit, as she lights up. "I was sitting here thinking a beer would be nice, but I guess a joint will do." I take a drag.

"I needed one today," she says through a lungful of smoke.

"Why? What happened today?"

"Today is my thirtieth birthday."

"Wow, happy birthday, Nomi! Thirty is a big deal."

"Thanks. It's kind of a big deal for me. I used to imagine my thirtieth birthday, and where I'd be and how I'd celebrate."

"No birthday cake, no candles?"

"They made me a gluten-free cupcake in the kitchen, but we try not to make a big deal out of these 'special occasions.' Too much ego gratification."

"Because it's all about you?"

"Yes. 'Caught in a self-centered dream—only suffering.'"

"Another Suzuki quote?"

"No, some other Zen Master."

"Well, here's to you, kid." I raise the joint as if in a toast. "With this imaginary champagne glass I toast to your very special day, and to a successful year ahead with lots of blissful meditations. You deserve it."

"Thanks, you're sweet." She takes a deep drag from the joint and passes it to me. A relaxing feeling trickles through my body and makes me smile. This is better than a beer.

"If I had known, I would have thrown you a surprise party with streamers and champagne and at least one scantily clad stud jumping out of a cake."

Nomi laughs out loud. "I love that image. A scantily clad stud!"

"Shirtless, of course, with nice shoulder muscles—think Daniel Craig."

"You would have rounded up James Bond?"

"Maybe not in person, but a look-alike."

She's cracking up with laughter, so I continue.

"Very tight pants, barefoot—what shall we do about the hairdo? Do you prefer short cropped, or long? Blond or dark?"

"Stop it, Greg, my stomach already hurts from laughing!"

"Okay, I make the decision. I say longish blond hair, curly, of course, which he throws back out of his face with a seductive shake of his head. Smoldering green eyes fastened on you..."

She is rolling around the futon, holding her stomach, laughing. "God, I haven't laughed so hard in years."

"We didn't even get to the message yet."

"What message?"

"The stud is delivering a message. A singing telegram. Don't tell me you've never had a singing telegram before?"

"Never even heard of it."

By now, I'm feeling slightly light-headed myself. I jump up, tear off my shirt, and spread my arms dramatically.

"Nomi, Nomi,

The things you can show me,

The flowers you grow me

Your charms just blow me—away."

Oops, I got a bit carried away. She stopped laughing. I still stand there, shirtless, arms stretched out like an idiot.

She gets up quickly. I went too far. She's going to leave. But no—she steps up to me and starts to hug me.

"Hugs are good," is all I can think of.

"I was feeling so down, so depressed before I came here. Now, I'm much better; happy."

I pat her back. "Good. I'm glad. I was kind of low myself, before you came."

She starts to kiss me.

"Nomi, I don't know if this is a good idea."

"What?" She's pressing her body against mine.

"Nothing." I kiss her back. She feels soft and sweet. She's starting to work on my back and neck, her hands moving lower, down to my waist. I can't pretend I don't like it.

"Nomi, I don't think we should be doing this," I say with a lot of self-discipline.

"You don't like it?" she asks while her tongue is in my ear.

"I like it alright, but are you allowed to do this? Isn't there a rule against it for aspiring nuns?"

"I haven't had sex in years," she mumbles. "I thought I was okay with that, but it's my thirtieth birthday and all I got was a vegan cupcake."

"What about karma? This can't be good for our karma. It's certainly not good for my marriage."

She pauses, then pulls away. "Oh yeah, your marriage."

"That's kind of why I'm here."

"I understand. Just a kiss good night, and then I'll go."

Nothing wrong with a kiss between friends. I kiss her back with intensity, now that my conscience has been placated.

Another knock at the door. "Greg, are you there?"

"Fuck off, Hans!"

"Are you alone? Whose shoes are these out here?"

"I told you nicely, get lost."

Hans opens the door. No locks.

"Holy shit," he exclaims.

Nomi pulls back. "I was just leaving."

"It's Nomi's thirtieth birthday today. We're just having a little birthday hug."

"Greg, you have no shirt on."

"It's a long story, Hans. And you have no right to just barge in."

"I left my sleeping bag here."

"Take your freaking sleeping bag and get the hell out of here." I open the door, throw out his sleeping bag, and push Hans into the night. He stumbles on the stairs, cursing.

When I turn around, I see Nomi standing in the middle of the cabin, trembling.

I pull my shirt back on and face her.

"He's going to tell everybody," she whispers. "They'll kick me out."

Shit. Vega will kick me out too.

"I have nowhere else to go."

I run out of the cabin and catch up with Hans. "Listen, Hans, it was not what it looked like."

He grins. "I know what I saw."

That nasty piece of shit. The tattletale already ratted on Bill the Builder.

"You don't know anything." I have to come up with something fast. "She was depressed because it was her thirtieth birthday and nobody paid any attention. So I gave her a birthday hug." I know this is not good enough.

"That's not what it looked like to me."

"Hans, this has to stay between us." Hans, of all people, the worst rat of all of them.

He looks at me as if I'm crazy.

"Hans, what do you want?" I ask in desperation.

"I want constant protection. Around the clock. We're going to be like Siamese twins from now on, if you want me to be quiet."

Oh God, as if my life wasn't already complicated enough. On the other hand, if I'm always with him, I can make sure he keeps his mouth shut.

"How am I supposed to defend you? If Bill is really the murderer, I have no weapon to use against him."

"That's fine. As long as it's two against one, he won't strike. He's a coward. We know he doesn't have a gun."

I don't have a lot of options. "Okay, done." Anything to keep Nomi and myself out of trouble.

"Shake on it." Hans holds out his hand. "And you have to be a little nicer to me too."

"Asshole. That's not part of the deal."

11:30 P.M.

I'm lying on my futon, listening to Hans snoring full volume. I'm going to make his life as miserable as possible, but not quite miserable enough for him to rat on Nomi and me.

It's a real tangle. I need to tell Nomi not to worry, and hope she is not confessing our encounter out of an exaggerated sense of honesty. I don't know how to approach her, with Hans on my heels. The whole thing is messed up, especially since I tried to resist and took the moral high road. I don't deserve this.

8

Day 9: 5:30 A.M.
When the bell ringer runs by at 5:30, I turn on the light and shake Hans by the shoulders.

"Time to meditate," I shout at him cheerfully.

"Leave me alone." Hans tries to turn to his other side.

"Okay, I'm leaving. You can stay here by yourself and sleep."

"No, you have to watch me."

"That's not part of the agreement. You can come with me, but I don't have to stay here and watch you sleep. I'm not the one who's afraid."

Hans mumbles and curses under his breath, but he rolls off the futon and pulls on his pants.

"Dark, modest colors in the Zen-do, Hans," I warn him.

"Don't push it, Greg. I can still tell the abbot and your wife what I saw."

"And make a few more enemies. Of course you'll lose your protection as well."

I detect several inelegant words escaping Hans's mouth and set off with eager steps toward the Zen-do.

"You'll regret this," Hans grumbles behind me.

"Look at the bright side, Hans. This is going to be good for your karma."

"Karma, shmarma," he mumbles.

"Quiet now. Enter left foot first and bow." Hans needs a lot of coaching with the protocol.

When we are finally settled on our cushions, I hear grunting and moaning from his direction. I can't suppress a smile. If I keep this up, he'll stop following me around in no time.

As my breathing settles down, I consider all the human entanglements spread out in my mind: Nomi and me, Vega and me, Hans and me, Hans and Bill, Haku and Clarita, and on and on. Everybody is interconnected and attached to each other. No wonder the Buddha recommended non-attachment.

On the other hand, life would be really boring without attachments.

I'm getting used to sitting here in the mornings. I don't have any expectations of mind-boggling experiences anymore. I just want to take stock of my thoughts, my state of mind; the moment as it is, without my interference, one breath at a time. I can meddle all day, but during those forty-five minutes, I can let well enough alone. I don't have to change anything, I don't have to get anywhere, I don't have to achieve anything, I don't have to prove anything. This is it. No need to do anything besides being present. What a relief. I'm realizing that my special experiences during meditation don't really matter. They are just a little bonus. What really matters is simply to sit here. These morning hours have proven to be productive in an unexpected way. By declining to change or manipulate anything, I find that important thoughts emerge with clarity. Nomi said it will reveal itself. Maybe I'm getting an inkling about what she means. I have to contact her somehow, let her know that she's safe.

The bell rings and I look over to her seat on the floor.

She doesn't look up. I can't talk to her with Hans in tow. I can't call her, text her, or email her, but I can write her a letter.

7:30 A.M.

I amble over to the courtyard in the morning mist, Hans close behind. He's groaning and complaining nonstop. He still has a lot to learn. I feel slightly superior to his unenlightened state.

As we fill up with coffee, Bill appears out of the fog. Hans and Bill face each other.

"So you got yourself a bodyguard," Bill challenges Hans. "You big coward."

Oh boy, this is going to be unpleasant.

"What do you want, Bill? You want to kill me, like you did with the abbess and Jacob? Go ahead, do it right here, in front of all these people, all these witnesses."

"I didn't kill anybody. You know it and the police know it, so why don't you shut your big fat mouth!" Bill shouts.

"I saw you on the morning of the murder in the forest, carrying a big package!" Hans yells back.

"You and your lies! Spreading dirty rumors about stuff you know nothing about."

This is turning into a real shouting match. The other guests have formed a circle around us and I feel very awkward about being right in the middle of it. Bill and Hans are about to throw punches at each other.

The Ino storms down from the Zen-do, robes flowing behind him.

"Enough," he demands in a stern but tempered voice.

He steps between the two quarreling men and puts a hand on each of their chests, keeping them apart.

"This is a monastery, a sacred space. You will keep your voices down and behave respectfully. You are our guests; you have to follow our rules. No fighting and no raised voices are tolerated here."

Wow, he's a force to be reckoned with. Total control and total authority. I'm impressed. I feel the steely determination in the Ino's voice. It reminds me of the wave of contempt I felt from Haku. These guys have a quiet power that's stronger than anything I've felt in any boardroom.

Bill and Hans feel it too. They slink back, chastised, heads hanging low.

Abelli joins the scene. "What's going on here?"

The Ino just nods his head in the direction of the two culprits.

"With me, both of you." Abelli roughly takes Bill's arm, and Rodriguez, who's rushed up to his boss, takes hold of Hans. Together they lead them away.

I'm sort of relieved. I had a feeling things were coming to a head. But how are they going to keep them apart?

Rakesh and Mary walk over to me. They are inseparable now.

"That was tense," Rakesh remarks.

"Yeah. I'm glad the Ino stepped in. Quite a performance."

"He's good. I could use him at some of our department meetings at work," Rakesh says.

Mary smiles. "Or in the schoolyard."

"I guess it takes years to develop that kind of strength," I admit.

"What now?" Rakesh asks.

"I think they have to take one of them out, just like they did with Priscilla."

"Can they do that? Can they arrest one of them? I'm not sure they have the legal authority."

"I don't know, but something's gonna give."

～

10:00 A.M.

After breakfast I go to the library—without Hans, thank you very much—to write my letter to Nomi. I tell Nomi about my agreement with Hans, and try to assure her that she's safe. Hopefully, Hans is not spilling his beans at this moment. I add a personal note to express my friendship and respect.

I will always remember our encounters in the garden and your wise advice.

Maybe that's putting it on a bit too thick. I crumple up the paper and take another piece.

I have learned a lot from you, and you will always be in my thoughts.

I probably shouldn't start with the word "I," because of the ego and all that. She wouldn't like it.

Thank you for opening my mind to catch a glimpse of the world of Zen.

That's better. Suitably humble. Just "a glimpse," not implying that I understand anything, which I don't.

I fold the paper and address it to "Nomi." I don't have a second name.

At the office a new manager greets me. I guess the Ino got busy. It's a middle-aged woman with a shaved head. A full-fledged resident nun. Her name is Tomoko. She smiles kindly when I show her the letter.

"It's a thank-you note for a kindness Nomi showed me," I explain. "I don't know how to get it to her."

"Don't worry, I'll bring it to her room as soon as the Ino gets back. I have another note to deliver to Bill Mason."

Now *that's* interesting. I wonder who wrote to Bill. Or is it a phone message?

"Thank you very much," I tell her and bow. I know my Zen manners.

～

Outside the office, I sit on a bench underneath the wisteria trellises. It looks out onto a sliver of grass running along the main path. I have nothing else to do, so I just sit and wait for the Ino.

I watch people going by on their way to the bathhouse, or to the Zen-do or the dining room. The sun is out, putting a sparkle on the clean leaves of the oak trees, and the air is fragrant from wildflowers lining the path. They popped up after the rain. Blue jays are hopping and chirping in the branches. The day is starting out promising. What will it bring?

Time passes quickly as I sit and contemplate the scene. It occurs to me that I couldn't have done this a week ago. I would have been tense and impatient. Eager to do something. Maybe I have changed a little bit.

Before I know it, the Ino returns, and Tomoko exits the gift store/office with my letter and another note in her hand. Casually, I get up and follow her. She goes to the main building across from the Zen-do, where most of the monastics including Nomi have their rooms. It's weather-proofed for the long winter months, when the guests are gone and the monastic community buckles down for serious meditation.

I don't go inside. I don't need to know which one is Nomi's room, plus it would be suspicious. Guests have no business in the main building. I'm more interested in the other message. Tomoko comes out and walks down the path to the cabins, across the bridge. I follow.

A few cabins before mine, and two rows closer to the forest, she knocks on a door, but there's no answer. Tomoko sticks the note between the screen and the door frame and leaves.

I continue on the path as if going to my own cabin. Once I pass her, nodding with a friendly smile, I double back to Bill's cabin. I pull the note out and put it in my pocket. It's one of those phone message notes with the date and a time of 9 A.M.

on it. On a shady tree trunk between the cabins, I unfold it and read the short message:

Meet me at the Horse Pasture Trail before dark. I'll get you out. DB

My heart is beating fairly fast. I quickly refold the note and stick it back into the door frame. DB, Dick Baxter, Bill's boss, wants to meet him at the Horse Pasture Trail. I retreat to my own cabin.

When I arrived, Jacob, the office manager at the time, gave me a map of the hiking trails. Back then, hiking was still an option. I look for it in my drawer. It's a hand-drawn piece of paper, and the Horse Pasture trailhead is clearly marked about two miles up on the dirt road. I circle the spot with my pen and sit down to think.

Two miles is not far to walk from the monastery. But how would Dick Baxter get to the meeting from the other side? He'd have to get over the mudslide and drive fifteen miles on the muddy road. It feels fishy to me.

But it's a good day to go on a hike.

1:00 P.M.

At lunch—unremarkable soup and bread—neither Bill nor Hans makes an appearance.

I sit next to Rakesh and Mary. Dylan pours water.

"Where's Hans?" I whisper to him.

Dylan glances around the dining room to make sure nobody can overhear us. "In the back. They're keeping him with the kitchen staff," he whispers back.

Rakesh pretends to take a bite of whole-grain bread. "Bill?" he asks with his mouth full.

"In his cabin. They are not allowed to see each other." Dylan moves on and pours water for the guests at the next table.

Rakesh nods in my direction. "The Zen version of a restraining order."

So, if Bill is in his cabin, he must have found his note by now.

I'm excited about finally getting out of this compound. But I'm also wary about what I will find on the Horse Pasture Trail. Before I leave, I pocket my pack of Marlboros, a water bottle, and my baseball hat in my backpack and put on my good hiking boots. Ready. A knock on the door catches me as I'm just about to step out. Bad timing. Now what? I'm not supposed to leave the compound.

"Who is it?"

"Housekeeping. Do you need anything?"

I open the door and Tomoko stands outside. On the path, I see a cart containing two linen bags: one for trash, the other for fresh towels. Housekeeping is pretty basic around here. You can get new towels and get rid of your trash; that's about it. The rest is up to you.

"No, thanks, I'm fine."

"Okay, sorry for the interruption." She turns around and walks back to her cart.

How did she know she was interrupting something?

I take the back way, weaving through the cabins toward the dirt road. I have to pass the smoking area. *Rats.* Dylan is sitting on the narrow bench, smoking a cigarette. I can't get past him without causing suspicion, so I join him. He smiles at me and gives me a light. Feeling anxious myself, I can't understand his relaxed attitude and laid-back manner.

"How can you stand being so confined here?" I ask him.

"I'm just a volunteer. I can leave whenever I want. I'm not a monk or anything." He sounds content and in no hurry. I guess for Dylan the road closure and police presence hasn't been an inconvenience. On the contrary, it brought some excitement into his existence.

"Do you want to leave?"

"No, not at all. I'd like to stay for the winter, but I didn't work long enough this summer to be allowed to participate in practice session."

"You have to earn permission to stay for the winter?" I ask, dumbfounded.

"Yeah. It's a privilege to be allowed to stay. You have to earn your keep." He sounds regretful.

"Why do you want to stay?"

He takes a deep drag from his cigarette and watches the smoke curl into the air. "Because practice really helps me straighten out the confusion in my mind." He carefully extinguishes his cigarette in a tin can attached to the wooden enclosure. It's fire country here. "Okay, I have to go back to the kitchen, Greg. See you later."

I shake my head. What am I doing here? I'm surrounded by confused people!

Once he's gone, I sneak through the underbrush, past the parked cars, and join the dirt road up the mountain past the police guard at the gate. I'm just about to step over the narrow ditch separating the woods from the road, when I slip on a branch. It cracks as loudly as a gunshot in the quiet forest.

"Who's there?" I hear the police guard down by the gate. "Stop where you are!"

I hear loud footsteps coming up the path toward me. *Shit.* If I lie flat on the forest floor I'll make even more noise. I freeze and crouch. It's the best I can do. The steps are coming closer. I have to come up with a good explanation if he catches me. Through the branches I can see the green uniform of the officer. Can he see me yet? Another loud sound behind me startles me and the officer. "Show yourself!" he shouts. I'm still motionless, but a deer breaks through the underbrush and jumps across the ditch onto the road. In the middle of the path it stands stock-still and stares at the police officer. He already had his gun out and ready. "Jesus," I hear him say under his breath. The deer blinks. It is not used to human interference here at the Zen retreat. I have encountered several of them along the path, and they were not afraid. Just curious in a mild-mannered way. The officer puts his gun back into the holster. "Never mind," he mutters and turns around, heading back to the gate. *Phew.* Saved by the deer.

I hike up the dirt road. It feels good to leave the monastery gates behind and walk uphill. The sun warms my back. I smell the pine scent of the forest around me. Freedom. Take this, Abbess Clarita. Freedom is not always in the mind—it is in putting one foot in front of the other on a trail in nature.

Walking on the wide dirt road winding up the mountain, I feel like the only human soul in this forest. It's so peaceful. Two miles uphill, I reach the trailhead in half an hour. I'm a bit out of breath from lack of exercise and the altitude. No cars are parked at the turnout. Nobody is here yet. Unless they are hiding behind the trees?

I enter the shady trail, where I can't see farther than a few feet in front of me. The sunlight speckles the forest floor, which is covered with pine needles. It smells like Christmastime, when we first bring home the tree. Good. The pine needles muffle the sound of my footsteps. I stumble over a root and stub my toe on a rock. Yikes. With a shriek, a blue jay flutters up from a branch above. Twigs crackle and leaves swish. Another blue jay answers from afar. If anybody's here already, I've made enough of a racket to announce my presence.

My heart is beating too fast in my rib cage. I tell myself it's from the exertion, but I am nervous. If I'm correct, I'm about to meet a murderer. No movement. No reaction to the noise. I sit down on a tree stump to drink some water and calm down. Now I just have to wait for Bill Mason or Dick Baxter to arrive.

Hidden behind the trees and underbrush I watch the trailhead. It's cool and quiet. The minutes click by. It must be past 4:00 now, because the shadows are growing longer. The forest is vast. At first I thought is was silent, but the longer I listen, the more I hear: the faint crackling of branches, the wind in the trees, rustling of leaves, small animals scurrying through the underbrush, the whirr of an insect, the buzz of a bee, a woodpecker in the distance. The sounds and sights of a forest that's alive.

After about an hour, judging by the sun, Bill appears for his rendezvous with his boss Dick Baxter, who's coming to get him out, according to the note Tomoko delivered. Bill's wearing a backpack and a baseball hat. His arm is still in a sling. He's ready for his extraction. Bill sits down in the shade on a fallen tree trunk and waits. I can see him, but I have to make sure he doesn't see me. I sit as quietly as I can, summoning my meditation experience. It's hard. I shift on my tree stump to get more comfortable. The tree trunk's surface is spiked with wood chips and splinters. Not helpful to sitting quietly. I try to loosen my tense calf muscles, when I feel something crawling up my leg. It's inside my pants, tickling. I try to shake it out. That doesn't work. Instead, it starts to sting me. My left leg is itching all over now. On the forest floor before me, I see a low, round hill covered with small red insects. Fire ants! I jump up and stifle a cry. He must have heard me! He's going to come after me. It's just me, the fire ants, and a killer in this vast forest.

Footsteps coming up the dirt road save me. Bill must have heard them too. He looks confused. I know he expected someone to come from the other direction: Dick Baxter getting him out. Slowly the steps come closer. Bill jumps up. Someone is walking around the bend. I can't see who it is.

"What are you doing here?" Bill shouts.

Who is it? Who just arrived?

A voice is answering, "What did you expect, Bill? That Dick Baxter would come and fly you out with a helicopter?" I know that voice.

"How did you know?" Bill asks, bewildered.

"Did you really think your boss cares enough about you to get you out?" I can't pinpoint the voice.

"The message wasn't from Baxter, it was from you," it dawns on Bill.

"You've always been such an intelligent construction worker," the other person laughs. I know that laugh. I hate that laugh. It's Hans!

"How did you do it?" Bill asks, baffled.

"It wasn't rocket science." Hans snickers. "The security in this place is nonexistent. They put me in the back of the store to keep us apart. Remember, I complained about being afraid of you? From the back of the store I had a perfect view of the office through the screen door. When it was momentarily empty, I wrote the message on the phone message pad. Easy. The Ino thought it was from his substitute, that nun, Tomoko, and vice versa. She thoughtfully delivered it to your cabin."

"You son of a bitch," Bill swears. "Why would you do this?"

"Why, Bill? Because you're in my way. I'm getting rid of you, and this is the perfect way to do it. You took a little hike in the forest and there you unfortunately have a fatal accident, as you fall to your death trying to run away from your crimes."

"You bastard, you won't get away with this..." Bill charges at Hans, who pulls out a knife and holds it in front of him. My switchblade knife! If it becomes a murder weapon, I'm toast.

"Stop right there," Hans demands. Bill stops in his tracks. "I'm going to tie you up with construction rope, just like you did with the abbess."

I'm wondering how to intervene. Trying to ignore the increasing stings of the ants crawling up my legs.

"I didn't kill the abbess, you idiot," Bill snorts.

"I saw you hiding the Buddha."

"Fine, I did that," Bill admits. "And he's back and hardly damaged. But I didn't kill the abbess. I just diverted attention from her murder, so it wouldn't harm us and DB Builders."

"That was stupid of you and it didn't work." I hear Hans snorting contemptuously.

"It did work for a while. They thought the murder was a robbery gone wrong, instead of coming straight for us."

"Shut up, Bill."

I hear grunting and a struggle. Bill with his broken arm in a sling is no match for bulky Hans with my switchblade. I peek through the branches and see Hans sitting on Bill, who's on the ground facedown. Bill's moaning in pain. Hans has his arms twisted behind him and is tying them up with orange construction rope. What a nice touch.

"Why do you hate me so much?" Bill grunts, his mouth full of dirt.

"You treat me like a servant. I deserve your job and the promotion. I need the money and you ruined the entire project."

"Hans, be reasonable. We can work this out."

"Too late. Nobody will suspect me. I'll be back behind the kitchen in no time."

"You killed Jacob, didn't you?"

"He heard me arguing with Baxter. I told Baxter you ruined the development. I was angry. I told him you stole the Buddha. I thought he'd tell the police. It was the perfect setup. How could I know you had an alibi with your meeting that night?"

"You killed a man for nothing."

"You were going to get blamed for it."

"You're a monster, Hans."

They enter the forest trail, Bill in front of Hans, like a sacrificial lamb. Hans is pointing *my* knife at Bill's back. They are really close now. I can hear their breathing and smell the fear in Bill's sweat. I can't believe I let Hans sleep in my cabin for two nights. He could've killed me in my sleep—with my own hunting knife. That thought makes me furious. With what I hope sounds like the cry of a warrior, I jump out of my hiding place and tackle Hans to the ground.

"Run, Bill, run back!" I cry. "Get help!"

Bill scrambles to his feet beside me. Full of rage, he charges at Hans.

"You're no help, you're injured. Go! Now!" I grunt as I keep Hans down and try to wrestle the knife from him. Bill runs off. His arms are still tied behind him, but his legs are working overtime.

"Noooo!" Hans screams. "You idiot, what are you doing?" He twists around on the ground until he faces me. His huge hands reach out for my throat.

We roll around on the forest floor. There's an abyss on one side and a rock wall on the other.

Between a rock and a hard place.

"How'd you know I'd be here?" Hans asks between shallow breaths. His hands are on my throat, applying pressure.

"I read your note. Like you said, security is nonexistent in that place," I grunt. Of course I didn't know Hans would show up. I just followed Bill. But Hans doesn't need to know that. I have him pinned down beneath me.

"You meddlesome idiot. Why couldn't you leave well enough alone? Now I have to kill you too."

"Shut—your—big—mouth," I say and punch him in the face.

He groans. With a surprise effort, he breaks free and throws me off him. He's a big guy. I roll over and kick the knife out of his hand. It clatters down the hillside.

"It's over, Hans. Bill will be back with the police any minute."

"I wouldn't count on it," he hisses and lunges at me. He strikes my shin with his boot and I buckle over in pain.

"You nasty piece of shit." I straighten up and ram him against the rock face. "I'm gonna tie you up with your own construction rope until they haul you off."

I feel his body going slack beneath me. Good. He's giving up.

"Ahhh!" he screams and pushes me off with unexpected strength. I'm caught off guard. He shoves me hard with his foot—and I tumble down into the abyss.

I bounce off the side of the mountain like a tennis ball, trying to grab at branches that fly by my field of vision, too fast to focus. Anything to break the fall. Looking down makes me dizzy. It's a long way to go. Above me I hear Hans laughing. "I'm coming after you to finish you off!" he screams.

I hit a narrow ledge and manage to grasp a bramble. It cuts my hand, but I hang on for dear life.

My body comes to a halt, against a hedge of underbrush. I can't move my left leg, and my ribs and elbow hurt like crazy. If he comes after me, I won't be able to defend myself.

"I'm coming after you, Greg." I hear Hans's voice above.

I guess this is it. How did I get here? They say your life flashes before you when it's about to end. I think about our sons. I see Vega's face, her disappointment in me. I wish I could have regained her trust. Why did I cheat? Vanity? Ego? It's all a matter of cause and effect, as the Buddhists say. But this—this is too high a price to pay for my transgression. This is worse than I deserve. I take a deep breath. It hurts my lungs. I have to cough. It hurts even more. Will I ever see my sons again?

I hear another voice above.

"Stop right now!" the voice shouts.

It sounds like Abelli, but I can't be sure. Thank the gods and the Buddha. Not a minute too soon.

"Hands in the air where we can see them. You're under arrest, Mr. Becker!"

That's Rodriguez's voice. I hear grunting. Must be Hans.

"I'm down here!" I shout. Another coughing fit.

"We'll get you. Just hold on a minute longer." Mary's voice.

"We'll be right there, Greg." Rakesh is here too? How did they all get here so quickly?

"I can't move," I call out.

"We're getting a stretcher. Hang on—we've got you."

Rakesh and Rodriguez begin climbing down to me. I hear them swearing on the steep slope as they descend down the hillside. What if they're not going to make it? What if they fall into the abyss as well?

"Hold onto the brambles," I call out, which causes another

coughing fit. What if I can't hold on until they get here? I'm feeling dizzy, and the thorny branches are slipping from the grasp of my bloody palms.

I hear footsteps accelerating. Stumbling down the slope. One of them has lost control and is tumbling down the hill.

"Rakesh!" It's Rodriguez's voice, warning him.

"Help!" I hear Rakesh sliding, in free fall.

"Oh no," I moan.

"Hold on, Greg—hold on, Rakesh." Rodriguez sounds more panicking than assuring.

A body crashes into a tree, close to my location.

"Ah, fuck. I think I broke something. I'm here, behind this oak tree. It stopped me from going all the way down."

"Okay, Rakesh, I'm right here. Greg, I can see you."

I see Rodriguez's green uniform in my field of vision, between two tree trunks. Who is he going to save first?

"I can't hold on any longer," I cry.

Rodriguez is here, on my ledge. Finally. He pulls me away from the edge, closer to the rock face. My leg and ribs hurt like crazy and I scream in pain, but I can let go of the brambles and relax my body a bit. At least I'm not going to fall off the ledge.

"Greg, I'm going to have to leave you for a moment to get Rakesh. You'll be fine, right? Just for a moment."

I grimace and nod. Rodriguez makes a lateral move toward the location where Rakesh is wedged behind a black oak tree.

"Okay, buddy," I hear Rodriguez say. "We're just going to climb over there to your friend's location, nice and easy."

Supported by Rodriguez, Rakesh crawls more than walks over to my ledge.

We all slump down in relief and exhaustion.

I'm so glad to see them, tears sting in my eyes.

"It's going to be fine," Rakesh mumbles, but he doesn't look fine.

"Mary went back to the monastery to get a stretcher and help to haul you out. We're staying with you until they get here."

I nod, shaking uncontrollably.

8:30 P.M.

Mary, Abelli, and Dylan come back with ropes and a stretcher after dark. They wear headlamps for safety. After they let down the ropes, Rodriguez secures me on the stretcher. On the top of the hill, Dylan and Abelli tug the ropes to pull me up. I feel like the bones that weren't broken during the fall are crushed now. Rodriguez and Rakesh stay with me all the way, trying to ease the impact. Rakesh is limping. They carry me back to the retreat and deposit me in the small sick room behind the office/store on the narrow bed (not a futon, I'm happy to see).

"All in all you were lucky, Mr. Stern. You could have died. The nurse will patch you up for the night," says Abelli.

"Thanks you for pulling me out of there."

"Thanks for stopping Hans Becker from committing another murder," he says gravely.

"Where is he? I hope not in the room right next to me."

"Don't worry. He's under guard and arrest in a separate building. Hopefully the road will open tomorrow, so we can drive him, you, and the other guests out of here."

"That would be a relief. I hope I don't have to share the backseat with him."

Abelli smiles. "You took a great risk, Mr. Stern. You should have told us about your suspicions." Voice grave and serious now.

I nod, thinking that I had to prove to him I wasn't the murderer, but I don't say it out loud.

"You scared the shit out of us," he bursts out, his composure suddenly gone. "What were you thinking?" Angry now.

I sigh. "I guess I wasn't. I just wanted to get to the bottom of this."

Nomi rushes in with a burst of cold air from outside.

"We're not done yet. I need a full statement when you feel better." Abelli's face looks grim as he nods to me and leaves the room.

Nomi stands at the door, looking at me, eyes wide. "Greg, what's going on? What did you do?"

"I had to resort to extreme measures to see you again."

She grins lopsidedly and with visible effort. Then with a sigh of relief she says, "This is really extreme, even for you. Let me see your leg." She gently touches my shin and femur. A few days ago I would have enjoyed her touch, but now I cringe with pain. "Ouch, Nomi. I think I also broke a few ribs."

"Lie still. It's going to hurt to breathe for a while. They tell me you almost died." Her voice sounds shaky and she's squeezing her eyes, as if trying not to show her emotion.

"It was a close call," I admit. Might as well milk the situation for a little sympathy.

"The shin's definitely broken. I can make you a splint, but we have to get you to a hospital for a cast. I'll clean your wounds and patch you up for the night." She's getting to work on my leg, all business and nurse now. No more emotion. The moment passed. It's probably for the better.

"Did you get my letter?" I ask in a whisper.

"I did. Thank you. It wasn't necessary, but much appreciated."

'Much appreciated'? That sounds kind of cold. But I get it. She needs to establish distance. "So we're all good?"

"We're good. I learned a lot from you too." She looks at me with an intense expression.

"What did you learn from me? I thought I learned a lot from you."

"I learned that kindness can come in many different

forms. I learned that I still have some attachments to my former life, but that's okay. It's not enough to ever make me want to go back there. On the contrary. I realized I wouldn't make it out there anymore."

"I made you realize that?" I'm not sure if this is good or bad.

We're both silent. Suspended in our movements, Nomi hovering over my bed, me just slumped on my pillows, dead tired. There's a lot I'd like to say, explain, but I just can't get the words out. Maybe it's okay if it remains unsaid between us. And a lot did not happen between us. Unrealized potential. Yeah, I like that. I think that's a very Zen way of handling the situation.

"Meeting you was one big lesson, with an internal logic and necessity contained in it. As the Zen masters say 'Life is our only teacher.' Whether you knew it or not, you helped to reveal the lesson."

This is way above my pain-addled brain. I can't process it, but she said we're all good. So that has to be enough. "That's nice of you to say, even though I don't really understand it. You're talking in riddles again."

"Don't worry about it, Greg. I'm grateful. Let's just keep it at that."

I'm so exhausted, I just nod and close my eyes. She takes my uninjured hand and squeezes it softly. It feels nice, but not exciting or anything like that. "Do you want something to help you sleep?"

"Do you have morphine?"

"This is a monastery, not a drugstore," she laughs, but gives me some herbal powder with water.

"I'd like to call my wife."

"Of course."

∾

11:00 P.M.

She brings me the phone on a long cord from the office next door and then leaves quietly.

I probably won't see her again.

"Greg, what's the matter? It's late. Are you okay?" Vega sounds alarmed.

"I fell down an abyss and broke my leg and several ribs," I declare dramatically.

"Oh my God! Are you all right? What happened?"

"They patched me up for the night."

"Where were you?"

"In the forest, and I fell down a ravine."

"What the hell were you doing in the forest?"

"I followed Bill Mason and stopped Hans Becker from killing him and me."

"That's awful, Greg! Who's Hans?"

"One of the construction workers. He's in custody."

"I'm so sorry. Are you in pain?"

"I'm pretty hurt. I need to get to a hospital for a cast and X-rays."

"I'll come and pick you up as soon as I can get through."

"They may reopen the road tomorrow."

"I hope so. You could have gotten yourself killed!" I hear her sharp inhale and her voice sounds suddenly high pitched. "I can't believe you were in so much danger!"

"It was a close call. Hans Becker came after me." I can't help myself from bragging a bit.

She is quiet for a moment, and I hear her swallowing, as if fighting back tears. "I'm so sorry, Greg. I got you into this."

"It's not exactly your fault. I chose to go after them, which probably wasn't a very good idea."

She's laughing now, in a distressed kind of way. "I can't leave you alone even for a couple of days. You get into all kinds of trouble."

Oh good, I hear tenderness in her voice, and relief, and real concern.

"Right you are, Vega. Please don't send me off by myself anymore," I joke.

"I want the whole story, in every little detail, when I see you tomorrow. Did they take care of you?"

"I'm in a splint and they gave me something to sleep. Some herbs. I doubt it will take the edge off. I'll make it through the night. But I really do want to get home."

"Definitely. And Greg,"

"What?"

"You did it. You solved the murder."

"Well, at least one of them."

"What do you mean?"

"Hans confessed to killing Jacob, but not Clarita. And I tend to believe him. He has nothing to lose."

"Be that as it may, catching one killer is impressive enough. Go to sleep now."

I can hear the concern in her voice, and a wave of exhaustion washes over me as the adrenaline slowly ebbs out of my system.

"Yeah, I'm beat. Not to mention hurting all over."

"I'm proud of you. I love you. Get some rest. Good night."

That went pretty well, I think, and close my eyes.

9

Day 10: 9 A.M.
Propped up on several pillows, I sit up in bed in the exam room when Rakesh, Mary, Bill, and Dylan come to visit.

"Holy shit, man, you look like hell," Rakesh exclaims.

"Thanks, Rakesh, you look great too."

"We're so glad you're all right. That's all that matters." Mary sits down on the edge of my bed and holds my hand.

"Thanks to you I'm still alive, just a bit damaged." I wiggle my toes in the splint. "You came just in time," I tell them. "I couldn't have hung on any longer."

"It's all thanks to her," Rakesh says proudly, pointing at Mary. "When you didn't show up for dinner, Mary got worried. 'He's never missed a meal,' she said."

"She's right." I smile at Mary.

"So we went to your cabin and found the little map with the circled Horse Pasture Trail. We told Rodriguez and got some flashlights. We were already on our way up when we met Bill on his way down, still tied up with rope."

"I want to thank you from the bottom of my heart, Greg.

You saved my life." Bill sounds quite moved. His arm is still in the sling, but otherwise, he looks fine. At least he took a shower and cleaned up.

"You're welcome. I didn't know what to expect when I got up there."

"Neither did I. Hans confessed to the murder of Jacob, since we both witnessed his admission. Add to that, attempted murder of the two of us."

"But you took the Buddha?"

"I did. I confessed. When I found out about the death of the abbess and the rope on her lap, I wanted to divert attention from DB Builders. The monastery decided not to press charges, since the Buddha's back and undamaged."

"What about the abbess?"

"I didn't murder her."

"They believe you?"

"They have no proof. The rope is not enough."

"Hans?

"He denies it vehemently. Not that he has much to gain or lose by confessing. They already have him for murder and two attempted murders."

We're all quiet for a moment.

"I brought you some food." Dylan breaks the silence and offers me a piece of gooseberry pie wrapped in a napkin.

"Thanks, Dylan. That's really thoughtful of you." I wolf down the piece of pie. I missed lunch, dinner, and breakfast.

"What was it like to fall down that ravine?" Dylan asks.

"I thought it was the end. The minutes seemed to stretch as I was tumbling past trees and rocks, bouncing off the hillside."

"Did your life flash by?" Dylan wants to know.

"Yes, kind off. I saw my wife, my sons... I had to grab onto some shrubs to break my fall."

"And it worked?"

"Not until I landed on this narrow ledge. The shrubs had

thorns, and tore up my hands." I show them my bandaged palms. "But I had more important things on my mind than a few scratches."

"Your life," Mary exclaims. She's holding Rakesh's hand.

I nod. "I had to pull myself up by my arms. My leg broke when I bounced off the rocks."

"Ouch." Rakesh grimaces. "Well, this whole nightmare is over. Thanks to you we can all go home. They opened the road this morning."

A knock on the door announces the arrival of Detective Abelli, Osho Haku, and the Ino.

"Good morning, Mr. Stern," Abelli says.

Haku and the Ino bows deeply.

I try to bow back, but wince from the pain in my ribs.

"May we have a word?" Haku asks.

"Please go ahead. You can speak freely in front of my friends," I say graciously.

"We would like to formally thank you for stopping Hans Becker from harming Bill Mason and yourself, thereby saving another life, and solving the crimes committed at this monastery," Haku says.

"You're welcome." I look him straight in the eyes. No cold front today, but no warmth either.

"We just have a few follow-up questions before you leave," Abelli adds. "As soon as you feel up for it."

"May I ask in how much debt the monastery actually is, to make it vulnerable to a hostile takeover?" I ask Haku directly. His face remains immobile, but he nods to the Ino.

"The monastery is operating on a very small budget. We have limited expenses, but we had to take out a loan of fifty thousand dollars after the last fire to repair buildings and upgrade the bathhouses. We are generally self-sustaining, but we didn't generate enough income to pay back the loan," the Ino says.

"Fifty thousand, huh?" I look at Rakesh and raise my

eyebrows in a question. "Can I have a word with Mr. Paneer here for a moment?"

They bow and leave the room. Rakesh sits on the edge of my bed. "What's up, man?" he asks.

"Rakesh, I'm sure your last bonus at your company was at least twenty-five thousand dollars." He nods almost imperceptibly. "What do you say we both chip in and help this place out?"

He hesitates. His dark eyes narrow; the thick eyelashes flutter. "That's not exactly how I had planned to spend my bonus," he says.

I nod, but don't say anything. I don't want to make his decision easier for him.

"… but I'm in." He exhales, and his shoulders drop as he relaxes the tension.

"Good." I'm relieved, but not really surprised. I expected this reaction. "I was hoping you'd say that. I'm sure Mary will approve."

He smiles and gets up to open the door for the police, monastics, and Mary.

"We have an announcement to make. My friend Rakesh Paneer and I would like to make a donation of twenty-five thousand dollars each to the Zen Monastery to pay off the loan so the retreat is debt free."

A gasp runs through the assembled people. I see Mary squeezing Rakesh's arm, smiling broadly and giving him a kiss.

Haku turns red in the face, his famous composure crumbling. It's worth twenty-five thousand dollars just to see his expression. He bows very deeply. I can't see his face.

"Be assured of our deepest gratitude," he says when he comes up for air. "Your gift, Mr. Stern and Mr. Paneer, is providing us with peace of mind and the ability to serve many seekers and guests in the future. You will always be welcome as our honored guests here."

The Ino, Haku, and Dylan, who has a huge grin on his face, bow deeply in unison.

"Not to mention all the good karma," Dylan adds, smiling from ear to ear.

Haku gives him a withering look. He's just a volunteer, after all.

"Would you like to make this donation anonymously?" the Ino asks.

"No, you can put our names on it—right, Rakesh?"

"Absolutely." Rakesh is very pleased with himself, and Mary looks totally smitten.

I imagine Nomi's face when she hears that she can feel safe in this place where she found a home. She won't have to worry about being evicted back into the outside world.

An agreeable outcome. But we still don't know who killed Abbess Clarita.

PART II

GREEN GLEN

10

One month later; Los Gatos, California

Our backyard in Los Gatos reminds me of Nomi's garden at the Zen Mountain Retreat. We have the same pink flowers, zinnias, but I never noticed them before. Maybe I wasn't paying attention. Our garden beds really need weeding. Well, I'm not doing it. I'm still in the cast and have to use crutches to limp around.

Through the kitchen window, I hear Vega clattering around with the dishes. I know she's watching me, so I quickly turn a page of my *Wall Street Journal*. I don't want her to think I'm meditating. Okay, I admit, I have changed since my return from the Mountain Retreat, but not in the way she thinks. Falling down a hillside and almost dying will change a man. Makes you realize life is precious and appreciate it more, flowers and all.

It's getting warm out here; I need to go inside and get some water. Getting up the back steps and opening the kitchen door is still pretty challenging with crutches.

"Hey," Vega says. "Need some help with that door?"

"Thanks Vega, but I can manage." Okay, I'm a cripple, but I can still open a door.

"How's the garden?"

"Beautiful. I saw two hummingbirds, an orange butterfly, and the bees are going crazy over your purple flowers."

"Irises."

"Yeah, those." Irises—I never knew that name.

"Do you want to go to San Francisco next week, Greg?" she asks without looking up from her dishes.

"Sure, if you're driving. What's going on in SF?"

"A dedication ceremony at the San Francisco Zen Center."

"What are they dedicating?"

"An Amitabha Buddha statue."

"Another Buddha of the Western Paradise?"

"This one is standing."

"And you helped them find it."

"Something like that."

"I can't sit cross-legged." I knock on my cast. I'm not sure I'm up for a Buddha dedication ceremony.

"Don't worry, you can sit in a chair. And Cora will be there."

"She's coming from LA?" It'd be nice to see Cora. I'd like to ask her a few questions.

"Yup. I thought you might want to see her." Of course Vega figured this out herself.

"I'd like to talk to her about Priscilla."

"That's what I figured."

"Okay, let's go." Maybe it's worth sitting through the ceremony to tie up a few loose ends. I sit down at the kitchen table.

"You know, one of the aspiring nuns at Zen Retreat said something strange. She said that whatever caused the events around Clarita's death will reveal itself. I didn't understand what she meant. Nothing has revealed itself, unless you believe that either Bill Mason or Hans Becker did it."

"Hmm," Vega says, stalling for time. She always does that if she wants me to figure something out myself.

"I figure Clarita was murdered because of either greed or revenge. I can only see three possible scenarios: One, the killer tried to steal the Buddha statue and was interrupted. Two, DB Builders wanted her out of the way, because of her opposition to the resort project. And three, gang members from LA found out about her location and smuggled in an assassin."

"I think the cause goes deeper than that. But we'll find out soon enough."

Another one of her cryptic sayings.

"You really think so?"

"Give it a bit more time."

I hate it when she does that. Like, I'm not patient or wise enough.

"Vega, we can't just sit around and wait for the killers to reveal themselves. If I hadn't followed Bill Mason to the Horse Pasture Trail, he'd be dead by now and we still wouldn't know who killed Brother Jacob."

"Yes, you were quite instrumental in that revelation."

I sigh. Sometimes she's so exasperating. She can't help it.

Five days later, 9:30 A.M.

We're driving on the 101 North to San Francisco. It should only take us an hour. Traffic is light. I sit in the passenger seat, pushed back as far as possible, cast resting on my backpack. We're passing the exit to Mountain View.

"So, this Amitabha Buddha statue we're welcoming to the Zen Center. Tell me about it."

"It's a wooden sculpture from Japan, the Edo Period, which lasted from the seventeenth 'til the nineteenth century. He's standing in royal ease..."

"Vega, I don't want an art lecture. Why is this Buddha

important and how does he fit into the Zen philosophy?"

"You know that Amitabha is the Buddha of the Western Paradise."

"Yeah, and if you die with his name on your lips you go straight there, through the entrance on Mount Fuji, to join all the singing birds and glittering diamonds."

She laughs. "You don't sound impressed."

"No, it sounds like a childish superstition. It doesn't seem to fit with the strict Zen philosophy."

"Point taken. The Zen Soto School in Japan developed out of the Samurai Warrior Class, which influenced its formal teachings: the austerity, the *zazen*, the simplicity. Amitabha Buddha represents compassion and kindness."

"To soften the austerity."

"That's a good way to look at it. The Amitabha Buddha brings an element of love, compassion, and devotion into the Zen Centers."

I mull this over and close my eyes for a bit. "Is he worth dying for?"

"I don't know, Greg. Depends who you're asking. Even though I appreciate the Buddha statues for their artistic value, I wouldn't die for them."

"Me neither."

The skyline of San Francisco emerges in front of us out of the ever-present fog, which the young kids call *Karl*.

11:00 A.M.

Vega drops me off at the entrance to the Victorian building where the Zen Center is located. Before parking the car she watches me limp up the stairs with my crutches. Several members help me. I'm fine.

A few minutes later I enter the Zen-do. The space is lined by high, arching windows. They let in plenty of light even on a foggy day. Chairs have been placed on the wooden parquet floor, facing the front of the room, where two Buddha statues flank the altar. One of them is new. Well, he's new to this Zendo, since he is actually a few hundred years old, but in very good shape for his age.

I'm comfortably ensconced on a chair at the left of the meditation hall, my injured leg laid up on another chair with a pillow, when Vega joins me. I'm having an animated conversation with Cora, who is sitting next to me.

"Cora, it's good to see you," Vega greets her. "Thanks for making the trip and for making Greg comfortable."

"Mr. Stern and I are old friends from the Zen Mountain Retreat. I was just complimenting him on his cast," Cora says with a laugh.

"I know it's an attractive specimen, even though it's getting pretty grimy," I say, knocking some dirt off the white surface. "But I'm getting everybody's autograph, so I may have to preserve this thing somehow."

"I thought you couldn't wait to get rid of it." Vega sits down next to Cora.

We probably shouldn't be chatting and laughing so loud. Other guests and members glance at us over their shoulder with disapproving looks. So what.

Everybody falls silent, as the abbess of the Zen Center walks in with a dignified smile. She begins the dedication ceremony with a short speech, welcoming the *sangha* and the new Amitabha Buddha to the community.

Vega looks at me. She wants to see if I fidget. I won't give her that satisfaction. I can sit still as long as the best of them. Especially in a chair, leg propped up comfortably. This is the first time I've accompanied Vega to an event here at the San Francisco Zen Center. Usually she comes alone.

I'm determined to solve the mystery of Clarita's murder, but I'm not doing this for Vega, or for the Zen community. I'm doing it for me. It's part of my nature to solve problems and find solutions.

I give her a little grin.

We've had a good run, Vega and me. We're friends and partners, have raised two beautiful sons. We've explored the jungles of the Yucatán and remote cave paintings in the bowels of Baja together. We've discovered extraordinary art and exquisite restaurants in London, Paris, Madrid, and New York. And yet—it doesn't seem enough for her. She wants more—another dimension. I'm fearless and competent. I'm just not that interested in exploring my "feelings," or those of others around me.

I like to play the game of success and I like to win. But there are times when winning is not the best outcome. At the International Management Conference in New York, I won the attention of a young Japanese scientist. I hadn't really expected her to be so responsive, but once I realized she was attracted to me, I couldn't turn her down. It was a mistake. I should've been stronger. I admit I have my weaknesses.

Vega says she's over it, but that she couldn't forgive the breach of trust or the disrespect I showed her, and the young scientist, by assuming that this one-night stand wouldn't have any consequences. That's why she sent me to the Zen Mountain Retreat.

Unfortunately, I didn't have much time to ponder my transgression there because I got involved in a murder and a mudslide, and fractured my leg. I bet Vega had something more contemplative in mind.

The chanting around us ebbs and flows. There is a short silent meditation period and then a little bell rings. People stretch on their chairs or pillows. The ceremony is over. More bows to the abbess, the Buddha, and the *sangha*. We can go. I'm in no rush to get up. Let the crowd get out first. I need space for my crutches.

1:00 P.M.

Cora, Vega, and I sit in a booth at the Thai restaurant across the street from the Zen Center. We order spring rolls, satay with peanut sauce, and red curry.

"The food at the Mountain Retreat was so good," Cora sighs.

"Yes, until the mudslide and the food rationing. You were lucky to get out when you did," I reminisce.

"You had to accompany Priscilla back, didn't you, Cora?" Vega asks.

"Her name is Mrs. Howard, not Cora," I correct her.

"Oh, your wife can call me Cora, Mr. Stern."

"I see," I say, keeping any expression out of my face.

Cora can't contain herself any longer, and bursts out laughing. "I'm just messing with you, Mr. Stern. You can call me Cora, now that we know each other better."

I grin. "Then you have to call me Greg."

"It's a deal, Greg."

The appetizers arrive. After a few bites, Cora continues. "Priscilla was in a bad way when we left the Zen Retreat."

"How is she now?" Vega asks.

"Where is she?" I want to know.

"I can't tell you. She is in hiding from her past and the gang members she hung out with. I'm planning to visit her, to see how she's doing, since I'm already up here," Cora says.

"So she's close by," I conclude. "That means she is probably at Green Glen Zen Farm, half an hour north of here."

Cora looks at me sharply. "You'd better keep that assumption to yourself, Mr. Stern."

I nod solemnly. I know I'm right.

Vega has told me repeatedly about the Green Glen Zen Farm, trying to entice me to go with her. It's located in a coastal valley opening onto the Muir State Beach. They grow organic vegetables for the surrounding communities and health food stores. They are associated with the San Francisco Zen Center and the Zen Mountain Retreat.

"Don't worry, Cora. This is not going anywhere," Vega assures her.

"I've never been to Green Glen." Now that I think about it, it sounds nice: a beach, a state park, and a verdant valley.

"It's beautiful," Vega says. "Just a short walk to the beach, hiking trails along the coastline. "

"Maybe we'll go once my cast is off." I wouldn't mind checking it out for a weekend, since it is so close.

Vega looks at me skeptically. I've never expressed any interest in going to Green Glen before. But I've never had a compelling reason until now.

"What did you think of the ceremony, Vega?" Cora changes the subject, between bites of curry. She has a good appetite.

"Nice—simple and dignified. A good welcome for the new Buddha," Vega says.

Of course she'd say that. I thought it was a bit boring myself.

"Remember Abbess Clarita's funeral, Cora?" Now, that was *not* a boring ceremony!

"Dear Buddha, what a scene. Clarita's brother was so angry."

"You should have seen him, Vega. He was cursing and practically foaming at the mouth, because the monastery had failed to protect his sister."

"His reaction is somewhat understandable. He lost his sister twice: first to the witness protection program, then to a killer. I hope the community has found some peace after all the turmoil." Vega takes a sip of tea.

Always sooo understanding.

"Thanks to your husband's donation, at least they don't have to worry about losing the property anymore," Cora says.

I'm squirming, a bit embarrassed. I don't want to talk about it. I know the donation was extremely generous, but it was also a power play. Now Osho Haku owes me. Of course Cora knows this too, which is why she has a wicked grin on her face. Vega puts her hand on my arm and smiles. No matter the motivation, the donation is helping the monastery and its members. That's what's most important to her.

We have finished and offer to give Cora a ride, but she has transportation lined up at the Zen Center. We watch her walk across the street. Vega leaves to get the car, and I pay the bill.

3:30 P.M.

In the car on the way back, we get stuck in traffic. Of course, the southbound 280 Freeway is a parking lot at this time of day.

"So you want to go to Green Glen?"

"Let's do it. Their food must be pretty good, if they have their own organic farm."

"You don't want to go there for the food. You want to talk to Priscilla."

"I do. But I don't know if she'd talk to me. I didn't have much luck at the Zen Retreat."

"She's traumatized and in hiding," Vega considers.

"She might be more responsive talking to a woman." I need Vega's help with this. "Let's both go. So, if there is another catastrophe, such as a mudslide or an earthquake, at least we're in it together," Vega says.

"How about a beached whale or a tsunami?" I suggest.

"How about a nice, quiet, meditative and contemplative stay?"

Sounds boring to me. Not my style.

The traffic is moving another twenty feet ahead. We are making progress, a little bit at a time.

11

———

Three weeks later

We're back in the car, going north to the Green Glen Zen Farm. My cast is off and I'm happy to be back in the driver's seat. Vega sits next to me and watches the landscape flow by. It's fall, but you can barely tell here in the Bay Area. Some trees turn a pale shade of yellow, some lose a few leaves. That's about it.

"I miss the change of seasons I was used to on the East Coast. Colorful signs of the passage of time; the approach of darkness and introspection," she says. "I want to go to the mountains to see the fall colors."

"Which mountains?" I have no idea what she's talking about.

"I don't know. Don't the aspen is New Mexico turn golden this time of year?"

"You want to go to New Mexico? Maybe we'll see some fall color in Green Glen."

"I doubt it."

"I can't go to New Mexico. I've taken off too much time from work already. Now we're taking two days to come up here. I need to catch up." *Someone has to make some money in our family.*

"It was your idea to go to Green Glen to talk to Priscilla, not mine. Plus, we're only going for a weekend," Vega reminds me.

I'm not answering. I'm slightly annoyed. She should be happy I'm willing to go to Green Glen with her. But it's never enough. All I'm saying is I don't have time to go to New Mexico this fall.

12

Green Glen, Day 1: 4:00 P.M.

The wooden Japanese-style guesthouse is simple and elegant: two stories arranged around a spacious central atrium, with a kitchen and sitting area. We have a double room on the second floor with real beds (not futons), a desk, a balcony looking into the trees, and a bathroom to be shared with the room next to us. Very civilized. I can't complain.

6:00 P.M.

People sit silently in the dark, subterranean dining room, looking kind of glum. Nobody is allowed to eat before the Zen Masters enter. These are the half dozen senior monks and nuns who have risen through the ranks at Green Glen, have received transmission, and achieved the highest level of accomplishment in the Zen hierarchy. In short, Zen royalty.

I look at the large bowls of salad, grains, and sauce on a table in the front of the room.

"That doesn't look very appetizing," I whisper.

"Shhh," Vega hushes me.

I make a face.

The double doors of the dining hall open and in they sweep. Black robes flowing, hands folded in front, serious and without making eye contact, they stride across the room with large, purposeful steps. We bow. They bow, not as deeply. They start to serve themselves and we form a line behind them.

I spoon brown rice, kale salad, and vegetables on my plate, raising my eyebrows. "This is it?"

"Quiet," Vega hisses.

Back at our table, we begin to eat. Nobody speaks. Here at Green Glen they observe silence during meals. Everybody is bent over their bowls, chewing slowly. The Zen royals have their own table, of course.

Vega notices that I'm just about to explode, so she points her chin toward the bowls and then at the door. Relieved, I nod. We pick up our food bowls and utensils and go outside.

As soon as the door closes behind us, I erupt. "This is awful. It's dark and dingy and the silence is oppressive."

"Pull yourself together. Let's sit over there at the picnic bench," Vega suggests.

After a few bites, I continue. "Why can't we talk and get to know our fellow guests like at the Mountain Retreat?"

"This is different."

I'm a gourmet cook. I've made some of the dishes from the Zen Mountain Retreat cookbook for Vega since I got back. Eating is one of the great pleasures in life, so this bothers me.

"Why is it so different if both centers are part of the same umbrella organization? Cooking was considered a meditative practice at the Mountain Retreat."

"Each center has autonomy. Did the monastics eat with the guests at the Mountain Retreat?" she asks.

"No, I guess they ate separately," I admit.

"There you go."

So I guess that means if we had eaten together, everybody

would have had to observe silence there as well. I'm not supplying this conclusion out loud. I hate it when she applies the Socratic method of asking a question and letting me come up with my own answer.

"But we're guests. We paid for this," I say instead.

"Exactly. We are guests and have to respect the rules of our hosts."

I roll my eyes and drop my fork on the wooden table for emphasis.

"Have you given any thought to why they do it this way?"

She just can't admit that the food is bad.

"They don't want us to enjoy our food?"

"Maybe."

"They want us to focus on eating instead of chatting."

"Maybe. It's not gourmet, but it's nutritious. If you have too many flavors, it's hard to appreciate them all."

"Not for me. Don't they want to enjoy life?"

"That's a matter of perspective."

"Oh Vega, that's another one of those riddles they constantly gave me at the Mountain Retreat. Don't you start with those. I don't need another teaching moment."

We stare at each other. This is not going well.

"Excuse me, may I sit here?" A young kid with long, curly hair holding his dinner tray stands next to the picnic table.

"Please, take a seat." We both invite him, glad for the distraction.

"Thanks. My name is Alex." He sits down.

We introduce ourselves.

"Do you live at Green Glen, Alex?" I ask.

"I've been here for eighteen months, so I guess you can say I live here," he says between bites.

"You're a student?" Vega wants to know.

"Yes, and I work in the kitchen. I helped to cook your meal."

I make a face, and Vega shoots me a warning glance.

"It's pretty dark in the kitchen," Alex says. "I need some fresh air after working inside for hours."

I open my mouth, but before I can get a word out, Vega jumps in quickly. "We hear you. It's nice to have a conversation."

"Oh, the silence. Yeah, you're supposed to eat mindfully."

"Alex, do you know a young student, or apprentice, named Priscilla, who came here about a month ago?" Enough chitchat. Let's talk about something substantive.

Alex pauses, thinking. "No, I don't think so. Sorry."

Most likely she changed her name.

"She's petite, dark skin, big eyes, skinny, and very shy," I continue.

Vega punches me in the side with her elbow.

"She's not a student or volunteer. She may be in seclusion. I might have seen her at morning meditation once or twice."

"We'll be there tomorrow morning, so we can see for ourselves," Vega says quickly, before I can ask this kid any more questions.

"How long are you here?" Alex asks.

"Just for the weekend."

"That's short, but this place is always a sanctuary. I'm grateful I found it." Alex smiles and motions to the shady trees overhead, to the valley with the gardens and farm beds opening out in front of us, leading to the beach.

"Yes, it's beautiful." Vega takes a deep breath. Finally she's relaxing a bit.

Alex has finished his meal and is getting up. "I gotta go back. I'm helping with cleanup. Enjoy your stay." He bows and takes his tray.

"Thanks for sitting with us, Alex," Vega calls after him.

He turns around and smiles.

It's back to just Vega and me. Hopefully this excursion is going to improve from here on in.

~

7:00 P.M.

"Let's take a walk to the beach and watch the sunset," Vega suggests.

"Maybe we can find a restaurant along the way."

We deposit our bowls in soapy water in the dining hall and I sweep the room with a contemptuous glance. Nobody pays any attention. Back outside, we find the main path and follow it through the gardens and vegetable beds to the beach.

"Alex seems like a nice kid," Vega says to break the silence.

"He seems a little lost."

"That's why he's here."

The cool evening air carries salty traces from the ocean ahead of us behind the dunes, and we glimpse the orange rays of the setting sun.

"What about these Zen Masters? They look pretty arrogant." I know it's childish to harp on the food and the attitude of the Zen Masters, but I just can't let go.

"What makes you say so?"

"The way they swept into the dining hall and everybody had to stand and bow."

"They own this place."

"Literally?"

"It's part of a foundation, but they built this center. They constructed the buildings, run the farm, plan all the guest programs, and they give refuge to people like Alex and Priscilla."

"With all that competence, power, and self-discipline they could accomplish a lot in the outside world."

"They *have* accomplished a lot. They built an international network of Zen Centers."

"You know what I mean."

"Maybe you have a very narrow definition of success."

"To be successful in any profession, you have to put in your ten thousand hours of practice. It's not just about meditation."

"But it's much harder to conquer the mind than the stock market."

"Don't underestimate the stock market."

"I won't, but you shouldn't underestimate the power of meditation. By the way, how did you come up with the number of ten thousand hours?"

"Someone at the Zen Retreat told me."

"Who?" she asks.

"A student." She doesn't need to know it was a female student.

The winding path reaches its end. The inlet of Muir Beach, studded with rugged rocks submerged in windswept water, opens up in front of us. It's dipped in gold.

"The food was pretty bad," Vega admits and takes my hand. "But this is glorious."

We stare at the flaming sky together.

13

Green Glen, Day 2: 5:30 A.M.
No bell ringer runs through Green Glen in the morning. There's just a distant ring and a subtle clack signal of the wooden boards calling us to meditation. It's easy to miss.

Vega shakes me gently and asks, "Do you want to sit *zazen?*"

I get up right away without complaint.

The Zen-do is impressive. Several levels of platforms accommodate the sitters. Guests like us are not encouraged to attend, and the etiquette is rigorous, but we are tolerated, if we insist. We wait outside the door until the Zen Masters have entered in intimidating formation. Somehow we make it to our seats without stumbling or otherwise embarrassing ourselves.

We sit in the second row, facing the backs of Zen Masters who face the wall. The wooden clacks accelerate. The shifting, fidgeting, and coughing stops. All sound is absorbed by rhythmic breathing, in and out, in unison.

I like the moment when the restlessness ceases, when stillness and peace spread like a gentle wave. Nothing to do. Nowhere to go. I have arrived. I focus on my breath, and try to watch the thoughts come and go without judgment. I want them to arrive and leave like visitors who have no power to pull me along with them.

It's hard to stay focused on the simple observations of the sounds, smells, and sense perceptions in the Zen-do, but I keep trying: the feeling of the cool morning air, the cushion under me, and my bare feet on the wooden platform; the first, timid birdsongs of the morning; the smell of wood and burning candles. The sensations pass by like a parade, as long as I don't react, and don't give them too much attention. I still get distracted, but I'm getting better at acknowledging my fears, expectations, confusion, and doubt, and hold them in awareness. The time between thoughts and feelings extends, and slowly the inner space expands. It's not an escape from life, but an acceptance of all its manifestations inside and outside of my mind.

The powerful focus of the Zen Master in front of me elevates my own awareness.

7:00 A.M.

On our way to breakfast, a sigh escapes me.

"That bad, huh?" Vega asks.

"No, it was nice. I like meditation, even though I'm still not that good at it."

"That's why it's called practice," she says. "Did you see Priscilla?"

I expected her to comment on my meditation 'practice', but she let it go. Good. I'm not doing it for her. I'm doing it for myself.

"It's hard to recognize anybody when they face the wall. I may have spotted her during walking meditation at the break. I'm not sure it was her, though. I only saw her from the back."

I hesitate before the door of the dining room. "How about we walk into the little town by the beach and have breakfast there?"

Vega peeks through the glass windows. "Green Glen is famous for its fresh-baked bread. But they don't serve it in the dining room. I think there's some in the kitchen of our guesthouse. Let's go check," she says.

We walk back to the Japanese-style building between the trees. The wide-open interior, with its central potbelly stove and simple wooden furniture, is spacious and inviting. Sure enough, in the communal kitchen we find a fresh, crunchy loaf of wholewheat bread in the cupboard, and butter and jam in the fridge.

Feeling like two kids playing hooky, we eat with relish.

"How are we going to contact Priscilla?" I ask Vega between bites.

"If she's in seclusion, it will be impossible to talk to her."

"We came all this way, and we're so close. We gotta make this happen."

"We actually didn't come that far. It was less than an hour's drive. I don't have any clout here. Unless we meet her by chance, it would be best to just enjoy the weekend without being fixated on Priscilla."

I ignore Vega's comment. I have to come up with another way to find Priscilla.

The entrance door opens and two new guests arrive with their duffle bags. They step into the building's atrium and I jump up in surprise.

"Rakesh, Mary—what are you doing here?"

The two newcomers drop their bags and we hug.

"Vega," I gesture to her, "this is Rakesh from Silicon Valley, and Mary, one of Clarita's followers at the Mountain Retreat? They were my partners in crime-solving from the

Mountain Retreat. They pretty much saved my life, when they climbed the Horse Pasture Trail to find me."

Rakesh and Mary grin at the memory.

"Rakesh, Mary, my wife, Vega." They shake hands.

"What a coincidence," Vega says. "Are you here for the weekend?"

Actually it is quite a coincidence. What are they really doing here? I suspect they have an ulterior motive, just like me. After all, Mary knew Priscilla well.

"Yes, we're here just for two days—escaping the city, hiking, meditating," Rakesh says with his arm around Mary.

They look very much in love. I guess murder, a torrential rain storm, and a mudslide had at least one positive outcome —these two found each other.

"You missed morning meditation and breakfast—nothing to write home about there. Want to join us for a hike along the coast?" I suggest.

"Sure," he says. "We're just going to drop off our bags."

It turns out they are in the room next to ours.

10:00 a.m.

We are climbing the coastal trail from Muir Beach toward Pirates Cove. Rakesh, Mary, and I discuss our adventures at the Zen Mountain Retreat. Vega quietly takes in the breathtaking views. From a plateau high above the coast, we can see the top tier of the city, and the towers of the Golden Gate Bridge emerging through the fog.

"This is like the grand view of life, the big picture you can only see from afar and from above; a wide horizon instead of a narrow linear path," Vega observes.

We sit under a tree in the shade for a drink of water. The fog can't reach us here.

"I know Priscilla's here," Mary says.

"I think you're right. But we may not be able to talk to her. She's in hiding," I say.

"I'm an old friend." Mary looks into the distance as if she could find Priscilla there.

"Maybe you'll have more luck than us." I hope so.

"I *have* to find her and talk to her." Mary takes a long drink from her water bottle and gets up.

"Why is it so urgent, sweetheart?" Rakesh asks kindly. "Can't we just enjoy the scenery?"

I'm with Mary. Who cares about the scenery if there's a murder to be solved?

"There's something I have to resolve. Until then, I can't relax and enjoy the view." Mary sounds stressed; the brows in her classical Nefertiti face are wrinkled. What's worrying her?

"Can you tell us what bothers you so much?" Rakesh asks. "Maybe we can help."

"It's complicated. I should have said something a lot earlier." Mary shakes her head. Suddenly she starts to sob, her face buried in her hands.

We stare at her, taken aback, unprepared for this outburst. Vega sits down next to Mary on the log and puts her arm around her.

"It's okay, Mary. I don't know what's going on, but it's probably not as bad as you think," she says in an effort to comfort her.

Rakesh sits on her other side with a helpless expression.

"It is bad—it's worse than you can imagine," Mary sobs.

"Something happened at the Mountain Retreat, something involving Priscilla?" Obviously.

Mary nods. "I saw her."

"Where and when?" Finally we're getting somewhere.

"The morning we found the abbess."

We freeze in mid-motion. Rakesh sits up straight, as if an energy bolt went through him. "Tell us what happened."

Mary sniffs and nods. "I went to the Zen-do early that

morning. I was up before the bell ringers. I saw Priscilla coming out of the meditation hall. She looked confused, disturbed. I don't know if she even recognized me; she seemed to look right through me. Then she turned and ran into the forest in the back of the Zen-do."

"Why didn't you tell anybody?" I ask.

Another sob shakes Mary's body. "I didn't know what to do. Priscilla was so vulnerable. I couldn't see her as a murderer. I told myself that she must have found the dead abbess and that's why she was so disturbed and in shock."

"Maybe that's exactly what happened," Rakesh says.

"You need to tell the police." I'm adamant.

"I can't—it's too late now," Mary wails.

"It's okay, Mary, we'll figure it out," Rakesh says, trying to calm her.

"The longer I waited, the more worried I became. What happened in the Zen-do that morning? I still can't believe she would hurt Clarita, but I started to have doubts. Maybe someone was pressuring her. And then after her outburst in the yoga center that night..."

"We need to inform the police," I press on.

"Don't you understand, Greg? If Mary goes to the police now, she'll be charged with obstruction of justice, with-holding information, lying to the authorities. She'll incriminate herself." Rakesh has taken a protective stance between Mary and me.

I shake my head. This is no time to be protective. The information needs to be made available to the police. Now.

"Let's talk to the abbess first. She'll know what to do," Vega finally says.

"Oh yeah? In their infinite wisdom the Zen Masters will solve the entire dilemma?" I'm no fan of the Zen Masters.

"Don't let your ego and aversion get in the way of the truth," Vega admonishes me.

The Zen answer to every problem: the ego did it! But facts have nothing to do with ego.

"In what way are the Zen Masters qualified to conduct this investigation?" I want to know.

3:00 P.M.

As usual, Vega tries to defuse the tension. "Let's just walk back, and calm down, and meditate on the right way forward."

"But which one is the right way?" I look around, confused about the direction back to Green Glen. We're at a crossroad, with four different paths to choose from. I remember the path we came on, but the network of trails winds through meadows and canyons. It's really hot and we finished all our water. How far away from Green Glen are we?

"I don't know, I think we should go left here," Vega says. She looks hot and confused.

"No, right, going north along the shore line," I point in the opposite direction.

"If we go that way, we'll have to climb down this steep cliff to Pirates Cove and then back up on the other side. I'm not sure I'm up for that," Mary admits.

"Just give me a second," Rakesh says. "I saw the map at the trailhead, and I have a photographic memory. If the Pirates Cove is down this way, then the trail back to the Zen farm is this one right here in the middle."

"Thank the Buddha for your photographic memory," Mary says, relieved, and takes Rakesh's arm.

After a silent walk back to Green Glen along the beach and through the organic garden, we return to our separate rooms. The walls are thin redwood. We have to be careful what we say. Not an easy task, because immediately, Vega and I are arguing.

"We need to notify the police," I insist again.

"Fine, but first let's talk to the Zen Masters. We're on their property. We owe them at least that much courtesy. They may suggest a solution," she tries to argue.

"Are your precious Zen Masters above the law? What do you mean 'suggest a solution'? They have to bring in the police—that's all there is to it."

"Just give me one day. Let me talk to the abbess today, and then we can go to the police tomorrow. Please, think of Mary. She confided in us. We should at least respect her, and give her a day to figure out what she wants to do."

"Mary's waited long enough. She doesn't need another day. The sooner she comes forward, the better. It'll look better if she takes the first step."

Vega sighs. "It sounds like you want to take the step for her. Can't you understand her point of view at all?"

"Vega, we can't protect a potential murderer. If we do, we incriminate ourselves."

"One day. Just one day, please?"

I shake my head and step out onto the balcony, as Vega slips out of the room.

4:30 P.M.

Alex and I are sitting at the picnic table on the wooden deck. He's telling me about the seclusion cabins dotting the hillside. Practitioners can stay there in splendid isolation for as long as they need. I bet Priscilla is in one of them. Vega walks up to us. She looks glum.

"Vega, come join us. We're just having a cup of coffee." I hold up my mug.

She sits down. Alex has to go back to the kitchen.

"How'd it go with the Zen Master?" I ask.

"What do you think?"

"She gave you the glacial treatment, blocked you like a long-pole lacrosse player."

"Yeah, that's pretty much it, except I don't know about the lacrosse reference."

"I got one of those treatments by Osho Haku at the Mountain Retreat."

"I told her about the witness without mentioning her name. In response, she said that most things are not as urgent or important as they may seem."

"That was helpful," I say sarcastically.

"She looked at me with eyes like laser beams. I wanted to argue, but I couldn't. I opened my mouth, but nothing came out. I wondered if this mind trick would work on the police. I tried to assure myself that I'm not the enemy."

"How'd you break the spell?" I remember my meeting with Haku only too well.

"She did it. She blinked and told me not to worry—that they are not hiding anything from the police."

"Really? Nothing to hide?" I refrain from mentioning that I told her she wouldn't accomplish anything by running to the abbess.. "Why are there so few Zen abbots anymore? Mostly Zen abbesses?"

"What's wrong with women in positions of power?" Vega says defensively.

"Nothing at all. It's great that women are taking over. They are much more reasonable and kind. Absolutely."

"Okay. So why are you in such a good mood?"

I open my mouth, but before I can say something, the peace and quiet of the valley are interrupted by loud, cracking explosions.

5:00 P.M.

I react instinctively, pulling Vega underneath the bench. "Gunshots," I hiss. "Stay here, under cover," I order, and take off in crouched position in the direction of the shots.

My adrenaline is kicking in. It's like an automatic

response from my days as a police officer in southeast LA. My senses are hyper-alert, taking in everything at once. The breath comes hard and sharp. My body goes into fight mode. I assess the situation. There is no gate, just a short driveway from the road into the compound. Anybody can get in. I hear loud voices and more crackling shots in short succession. They sound like they're coming from an automatic weapon. Probably an assault rifle.

The scene in front of the Zen-do around the corner of the building confirms my appraisal. Three armed men, two with handguns, and one in the middle holding an automatic rifle. I do a double take. One of the men flanking the central shooter looks familiar. Where? The three point their weapons at a dozen people milling around in front of the Zen-do before dinner. They are caught between the three assailants and the meditation hall.

"Facedown on the ground, all of you!" the African American male with the assault rifle yells. Some people in the group whimper, gasp, or sob in response. But most of them obey and lie down. "No, please don't," a woman pleads. It's Mary.

"Leave her alone! Take me instead." The words come out of my mouth before I can stop them.

"Okay, you two over here, with me," the head honcho with the machine gun demands with a grin. Mary and I shuffle over to his side.

"Faster!" he yells, and lets loose another volley of shots. One bullet hits a man in the leg.

The cries, shouts, and moans from the crowd after this outburst obviously make the shooter happy, because he bares his extremely white teeth in a mirthless smile.

"Nooo, don't shoot!" Mary cries out.

I wish she'd be quiet and not draw attention to herself.

"Shut up and get over here, or I'll shoot you too. Kneel down with your hands behind your head."

I take Mary by the arm and lead her over to the head honcho's side, where we kneel on the ground. "Stay quiet," I whisper.

"Let's calm down and talk about this." I address the shooter with a steady voice.

"I told you to shut the fuck up!" Mr. honcho responds in an angry voice. Very angry. More shots in rapid succession. One of them barely misses me. I feel the heat zinging past my cheek.

"What's going on here?" the authoritative voice of the abbess cuts in, sharp as a samurai sword and unafraid.

"Who are you?" Mr. Honcho shouts back. A little less angry and a little less sure of himself.

"I'm Abbess Wu. I'm in charge here. And who are you?" She faces him directly, standing in front of the people on the ground, shielding them with her body.

"I'm asking the questions!" More shots in her direction.

"What's the purpose of this behavior? What do you want here?" The abbess doesn't even flinch. I breathe a sigh of relief.

"Finally someone asks the right question. You have something I want." Mr. Honcho sounds more confident again.

"We can talk about that. But first let these people go. They can't help you. Deal with me."

Laughter follows the abbess's statement. "Oh no, nobody's leaving. The more innocent people, the better. You probably have a martyr complex—like Dorothy, or Clarita as you called her. You're no use as a hostage."

He looks around at his companions for confirmation. One of them grins and bares his teeth. They flash silver and gold. "Sure, Drake. " he says. I've never heard his voice before but I've definitely seen him. His arms are covered in tattoos of strange numbers and symbols.

Clarita? Of course, I saw Metalmouth at Clarita's funeral. He accompanied Michael, Clarita's brother. Sweat is dripping down my back. That's how they figured out Priscilla was here..

I look across the clearing at Abbess Wu. The scene looks like something straight out of a *Star Wars* movie. Six Zen Masters flank and back Abbess Wu. All of them are dressed in long, black robes and stand in supremely straight, calm, and dignified poses. Arms folded in front of them, eyes unblinking. Between them and the three armed men, at least a dozen people are crouch, sobbing, some of them hurt, bleeding, others bending over them. Mary, another woman, and I kneel behind Drake, guarded by his two lieutenants, who are holding guns to our heads. The steel barrel behind me causes a burning pit of fear in my stomach.

"Let us take care of the wounded," the abbess says calmly. "They can go into the Zen-do. You and I will negotiate."

"Fine. Damian, go with them." Drake motions with his head to one of his sidekicks.

Damian waves his gun at the people on the ground, directing them to the Zen-do.

"Master Norbu will go with them. He is trained in first aid." The abbess nods to one of the Zen Masters behind her. He bows briefly and follows the group into the meditation hall.

"Faster!" Drake shouts, his voice high pitched and strained.

"These three..." The abbess points at Mary, the other woman, and me behind him.

"They stay!" Drake yells before she can finish her sentence. He sounds on edge, crazed.

"Fine." The abbess's voice is soft and soothing. "They can stay. Now, why are you here? What do you want?"

I hear a voice whispering behind the Zen-do. Hopefully, Vega is staying put under the bench.

"Someone's behind that building. "Find out who's there." Drake motions to his lieutenant behind him. "No police, or more people will die!" His voice snaps, as he shouts the last four words.

Metalmouth, Michael's friend, walks to the edge of the building.

"Let's resolve this peacefully," the abbess's voice interjects, unruffled.

"Ha, peaceful! It's too late for that."

"We are a peaceful monastic community."

"You are keeping one of my hoes captive here."

"Everyone is here voluntarily."

"She'd never volunteer to stay in this Jedi circus!"

"Drake, I got one!" Metalmouth shouts. "Get up," he orders someone behind the building.

My heart drops. What if it's Vega?

"Look what I got here." He walks around the corner, pushing Vega in front of him with his gun barrel. I flinch. In the pit of my stomach I feel a tight, hot knot of fear. Why couldn't she stay under the picnic bench?

"Kneel next to him," Drake points toward me. "What were you doing back there?"

"Nothing," Vega says.

"I heard you talking."

"I recited mantras."

The abbess raises her eyebrows.

"What the fuck are mantras?"

"Buddhist prayers."

I'm not sure about the mantra thing, but at least Vega keeps her eyes down on the ground. I don't want her to provoke him.

"You'll need those prayers, for sure."

She nods demurely.

"As we were saying," the abbess begins again.

"Before we were interrupted by this little spy here. Did you call the police?"

Vega shakes her head, trying to breathe and keep her composure. I look at her face, and her eyes are full of terror.

"Answer me!"

"No," Vega says. I hope she's lying.

"Are you Buddhists allowed to lie?"

"No," Vega says again, kneeling next to me. I shake my head in despair.

"Whatever. Another hostage can't hurt." Drake grins, flashing his white teeth.

"The person you are looking for?" The abbess is trying to redirect, to deflect attention away from us.

"I want Priscilla. Hand her over and I'll let these yuppies go."

Vega looks at me. I nod. Of course, this is about Priscilla. This is the man who kept her captive like a slave, as Cora had told us. He still thinks of Priscilla as his property. I send Vega a little lopsided, encouraging smile. We scoot a bit closer and our hands touch. At least we are in this together.

I look at Abbess Wu in front of her semicircle of Zen Masters—their shaved heads, floor-length black robes, poised expressions, hands in prayer *mudra*, thumb tips touching. I sense a slight alteration in their posture, as if they had all shifted their weight from one leg to the other at once. They are in unison. They are the complete opposite of the shooter, who is all adrenaline, uncontrolled emotion, rage.

"The person you are speaking of," the abbess begins, "are you sure she would want to return to you?"

"So you have her? You Jedi scum are keeping her prisoner. I knew it!" He turns around to Metalmouth behind him. "I told you, didn't I?"

Metalmouth grins, baring his glittering teeth, and nods.

"He was at Clarita's funeral," I whisper to Vega and nod toward Metalmouth.

Her eyes widen. Clarita, or Dorothy, as Drake knew her, was in witness protection at the Mountain Retreat, so it was an easy guess to figure out Priscilla would be here, since Green Glen is part of the same organization.

"Did you call...?" I look at her face and she blinks in affirmation. I'm sooo proud of her, even though a part of me wishes she'd stayed under the bench.

"No talking!" Drake snaps, and reloads his rifle, before he releases another volley of rounds.

Vega flinches and sinks down on her heels. She looks like she can't kneel on the stony ground with arms on her head any longer.

"Hey, who said you can go on vacation? Get up!" Drake yells at her.

She needs to keep it together, or this is going to be it.

Vega raises herself back up into a kneeling position, hands on the back of her head. I can see tears forming in her eyes. She's at a breaking point. I move closer and try to support her with my body. Fortunately, the shooter has shifted his attention back to the abbess.

"So you have her?" He laughs and turns around to Metalmouth. "Isn't that convenient? They can't lie! We should do more business with Buddhists!"

Metalmouth answers with a joyless smile.

"There is no woman named Priscilla at this monastery," the abbess states in a calm but firm voice.

I see a moment of confusion wash over Drake's face. But then he lights up.

"Ah, she is here under a different name. Of course, some police protection shit. No worries—I can describe her." He laughs again, looking to Metalmouth for an audience. "Petite, small tits, tight ass, black as sin, hair in a short afro. That jog your memory?"

"We are not cognizant of the physical attributes of our guests here," the abbess says. "We are concerned with their minds." She actually has a minuscule smile on her lips.

"Ah, the mind, the mind!" Drake waves his gun around in

a circle encompassing us all. "The mind's not gonna do you much good if I let the bullets fly! Enough with the games, lady. Go get her, or you'll be responsible for loss of life, and that can't be good for your karma." He turns and presses the gun barrel at Vega's temple. "This one will go first."

Vega looks like she's about to pass out. She can't take the tension any longer; a sob escapes her mouth and she falls down. I bend over her, cradling her head. "Vega," I whisper. "You can do this."

"Get the fuck back up. Or you're next," Drake yells.

I gently place her head down and withdraw from her. Where are the police? They should be here by now.

"Abbess Wu," a respectful voice interrupts. Zen Master Norbu bows to the abbess. "We need more supplies for the wounded people in the Zen-do. I need bandages and disinfectants."

The abbess nods and addresses the shooter. "We request permission to fetch medical supplies for the wounded people in the Zen-do. May I call you Drake?"

"Go right ahead. Your Jedi may go for supplies, under supervision, if he also brings Priscilla back here at the same time. No funny business. Ten minutes, or I'm gonna start shooting hostages. Got it?"

"Got it, Drake." The abbess nods at Master Norbu, who bows again and walks off in long strides. Metalmouth has a hard time keeping up.

"You guys sit down in front of me." Drake motions toward us. "So I can keep an eye on you."

We move in front of him and his machine gun. Mary, Vega, and I sink down cross-legged on the ground. Mary's eyes are wide with fear.

"Someone bring me a chair," Drake calls in the direction of the Zen-do.

"There's no chairs here, boss," his lieutenant, Damian, calls back from the meditation hall.

Drake sighs. "Wu," he orders. "Make it happen. A chair."

Abbess Wu inclines her head and one of the Zen Masters behind her peels off toward the dining hall.

Drake settles into the chair provided with a satisfied grunt. "Something to drink."

"We have water or tea," says the Zen Master still standing behind Drake after depositing the chair.

"Figures," Drake sighs. "Water's fine, I guess."

"So, now that we're all comfortable, what's your racket here, Wu?"

"We are a monastery and an organic farm."

"Now, isn't that wholesome! I'm sure Priscilla had a ball here!"

I hear police sirens in the distance. Finally.

"What the fuck!" Drake jumps up. "You'll pay for that!" He points the gun at Vega's head again.

She freezes. This maybe it. My wife, the love of my life, my one and only real friend and partner... I always assumed we'd grow old together. The blood drains from my head, as I lean toward her.

I hear the click of the gun's safety.

Vega is whispering, *Om Ami Dewa Hrihi*, the mantra of Amitabha Buddha. She squeezes her eyes together tightly—waiting for the impact of the bullet.

I slam my body into hers. We both fall over. Bullets fly, piercing the silence with the sound of death. I hear a moan behind me.

"Rakesh..." Mary screams. "My arm..."

"Mary!" a voice from inside the Zen-do answers.

Master Norbu returns with an armload of medical supplies. He rushes into the Zen-do. I see Rakesh running out with a first aid kit. He crouches down next to Mary. "It's okay, Mary. It's me—I'm here. I'll take care of you." His voice is heavy with emotion.

"Nooo!" another voice shrieks and a short, dark body throws herself at Drake.

The gun barrel lifts. "Ah, there she is," Drake says. "Come on, baby, come to your man. What the fuck are you doing here, you little whore? Why didn't you come back to me?" He pauses. His tone changes, turns sickly sweet. "You did good, baby! You finished off that snitch. I'm proud of you!"

Priscilla sniffles. Mary, Vega, and I gasp. The sirens grow louder.

"Okay, let's get outta here. We got what we came for." Drake turns on his heels, dragging Priscilla by the arm.

"No, I'm not going back with you." She presses the words out.

I can tell how much effort it costs her.

"What do you mean? Of course you're coming with me. I own you. You killed for me, and if you ever try to leave, you know what will happen. " Drake slaps her across the face.

She stumbles backward.

One of the Zen Masters steps forward between Priscilla and Drake. "This woman is under our protection. She doesn't want to go with you."

"Get out of my way, you Jedi filth, or I fast-track you to heaven, or wherever you Buddhists go thereafter!"

"Nirvana, and go right ahead." The Zen Master stands his ground.

"Are you nuts? I'll shoot you and then I'll still take her." Drake waves his gun at the Zen Master.

The sirens are very close now. I can see flashing lights in my peripheral vision.

"Drake," Priscilla interrupts. Even straightened to her maximum height, she only reaches midway to his chest. "I didn't kill Abbess Clarita."

"What are you talking about? She's dead."

"I didn't kill her. I didn't have to."

"What do you mean? Who killed her, then?"

A megaphone voice overpowers their conversation.

"This is the police. Put down your weapons. You are surrounded."

"Stay back or I'll shoot the hostages!" Drake yells. His voice has the crazy edge and high-pitched tone again.

"Let the hostages go, and we'll negotiate," the megaphone voice answers.

"Without hostages there's no negotiation!" Drake grabs Priscilla's head and pulls her toward him, pointing the gun at her. "Stay the fuck back, or I'll shoot."

"What do you want?" the megaphone asks. Out of the corner of my eye, I see a row of police officers in riot gear, pointing their guns at Drake. We do not want to get into that firing line. I shield Vega with my body and we both crouch as close to the ground as we can.

"I want to finish this conversation," Drake screeches. "Talk, Priscilla. Now!"

"Clarita had cancer. Terminal. She chose that morning to transition from this life to the next, making it look like murder, to save the monastery, and to save me!" Priscilla lets out a sob.

"What the fuck do you mean, 'transition'?"

"I can't explain it. She was ready to let go. She didn't want the developers to get the property. She told me not to worry. She was so kind, even though she knew I was there to kill her. But I didn't do it!" Priscilla's voice falters.

"You idiot!" Drake roughly pushes Priscilla away from him.

At that precise moment, the Zen Master standing behind his chair makes his move. With one foot he pushes Priscilla farther away, while simultaneously grabbing the gun and twisting it out of Drake's hands. Turning in a semicircle, he uses the machine gun to beat the pistol out of Metalmouth's hands. It flies into the bushes. Two other Zen Masters jump forward and grab Metalmouth's arms, rotating them to his back, immobilizing him. Drake is taken by a female Zen Master, her robes flying as she spirals around the shooter and ties him up with a rope she carried in her sleeve.

Nice moves!

Two more of the Zen Masters rush into the Zen-do. I hear grunts, a stifled cry, the shuffle of feet. Something clatters across the wooden floor. The shooter's gun? I get up and run inside. If I can grab that gun...

Inside it's total chaos. Damian dives after his gun. A Zen Master lurches after him. While they are on the floor, two hostages run outside, screaming in terror. Damian gets hold of the gun and points it at Master Norbu with a crazed cry. Norbu is on top of him. He can't miss.

I ram into Norbu from the side. We collide with a sickening thump.

The shot from Damian's gun rings out. It goes wide, toward the ceiling. Hostages throw themselves onto the ground, screaming. A Buddha statue on its pedestal tumbles over. There's a whack and the sound of a body slumping to the ground. Is it the Buddha or did someone get hit? Damian aims again. My stomach clenches. Another gunshot, this time from the back doorway.

A rough voice shouts, "Police! Hands on your head where I can see them!"

Everybody, including me, freezes in place. Even Damian. It's so quiet we can hear the click of the gun's safety switch. A body slams into Damian. Clatter and sounds of a struggle. An angry grunt. Damian's on the ground. A police officer stands over him, pointing his gun at the Damian's head. He's breathing heavily. Damian's gun falls out of his hand.

I grab it and kick it toward the SWAT team. I don't want to get shot by accident.

Two SWAT team officers, in full body armor, pull Damian up between them and drag him out of the meditation hall.

They must have sneaked into the Zen-do through the back door.

Damian's out cold. One of the officers holds his gun between my thumb and index finger, like a distasteful piece of rag. Hostages, helped by the Zen Masters, stream out into the open.

"The assailants have been disarmed and secured. SWAT team can now approach safely," one police officer reports into his walkie-talkie.

The abbess nods to her Zen Masters, and to me with the trace of a smile.

"They really are Jedis," Rakesh mumbles to Mary and Vega, in awe.

8:00 P.M.

We are huddled in the dining hall. The dignified silence has been lifted; everybody is talking, laughing, crying with relief. An ambulance has taken the wounded. The police have taken the three assailants. Alex and the kitchen staff brought fresh bread and fruit from the garden.

Vega and I are holding each other in a corner of the hall. We can't let go of each other. It was a really close call.

"You were so brave," I murmur. "You saved us, calling the police."

Vega shakes her head. "You saved me. I'd be dead without you. If you hadn't thrown yourself on top of me..."

Rakesh and Mary sit next to us. She's got a big bandage on her left arm, but fortunately the bullet just grazed her. She's smiling at Rakesh, who has his arms around her.

"The Zen Masters saved us. Did you see those moves? I couldn't believe it. They were like ninjas or something." Rakesh is still starstruck. "I've got a whole new respect for them."

"Me too," I admit. "But without the officers from the SWAT team we could've had a massacre in the Zen-Do."

"I'm glad that Priscilla didn't kill Clarita," Mary says with a sigh, while cradling her bandaged arm. "I didn't think she did it all along! Where is she anyway?" She looks around the hall.

"Priscilla is with the police for questioning, but she'll be fine," I tell her.

"She's finally free," Mary says.

"How did Clarita do that—choose the moment of her death?" I ask.

"Advanced Zen practitioners can leave their body at will. She knew she had terminal cancer. She realized that her death was of greater benefit to the community than her life," Vega says. "I've read of this practice, but it always seemed like something sages would do in mythic ages."

"But why?" Rakesh asks.

"She knew the monastery was about to be taken over by the developers. She knew, if she could implicate the developers in her death, the sale would be tied up in court. So she tightened the orange rope just enough to create an impression on her neck, then she transitioned. She saved the monastery and Priscilla," Vega explains.

"But wouldn't the autopsy have shown that she didn't die from strangulation?" Rakesh is still not convinced. His data-driven mind has a hard time accepting this scenario.

"It did," I say. "Detective Abelli confirmed it in our interview. The autopsy showed that Clarita's heart stopped. They figured it was a heart attack, brought on by the assault and attempted strangulation. They never assumed that the abbess stopped her own heart intentionally."

We sit dumbfounded, trying to process this. After a moment, I break the silence.

"To Clarita!" We lift our glasses of blackberry wine, which the kitchen staff has thoughtfully produced for the occasion.

. . .

10:00 P.M.

Walking back to our guesthouse, Vega says, "You know we really didn't solve Clarita's murder. We were just at the right place at the right time."

"Or at the wrong place at the wrong time. We almost got killed and Mary was wounded. Anyway, Clarita wasn't murdered."

"Yeah, I didn't see that coming."

I remember something Nomi told me about revelations. "Someone at the Mountain Retreat told me the cause and effect of Clarita's death would reveal themselves."

"She was right," Vega says.

"So, what did it reveal about us, our relationship? Did I, I mean did you... Are we okay now?" I'm trying to ask if she forgave me, but I don't know quite how to put it.

Vega pauses. "All I can say is that when I was kneeling there and you ran into the Zen-do, I was so scared for you. More than for myself. I couldn't imagine life without you."

"When Drake held his gun to your head and was about to pull the trigger, I felt that if he shot you, my life would be over too. At that moment, I didn't care about myself at all." My voice sounds shaky. It's true: at that moment I was nothing. I had no ego; I was just filled with the overwhelming urge to save Vega.

I look Vega in the eyes. They are filled with tears and emotion. The first time I saw these gray, I knew they were my destiny. "I'm sorry, Vega, for what I did at the conference. It was stupid, and thoughtless, and hurtful. I gave in to my ego and my pride."

Vega lowers her gaze. "Thanks for admitting that," she finally says.

It's something, but it's not quite forgiveness yet. "So, did I show enough regret?"

"It's not regret I was looking for. I knew you regretted it right away."

We stop on the path and she looks at me, not smiling. I'm squirming a bit.

"We've gone through life together, and we just went through a life-and-death scenario together. That puts things into perspective. It's enough to wipe the slate."

Okay, a clean slate. No conditions? "So I'm forgiven?"

She laughs. "I've forgiven you a long time ago. I love you, just the way you are. "

It doesn't always feel like that way, but I'll take it.

"You don't expect me to meditate every day?" I just want to be clear about this.

"Not unless you want to."

"I might do it, if it can be after five thirty in the morning." I roll my eyes and grin.

She bursts out laughing. "It's a deal!"

BOOK CLUB QUESTIONS:

1. Were you able to imagine the settings of the Zen monasteries, particularly the Zen Mountain Retreat?

2. Have you been to a retreat? Would you like to go?

3. Did the book introduce you to any Zen concepts? Were these intriguing or confusing?

4. Has this story increased or diminished your interest or curiosity about Zen Buddhism?

5. Could you relate to the character or Greg? Did you feel sympathy or antipathy for him?

6. This story is in parts about the relationship between Greg and Vega. Could you relate to that? In your opinion, would you give their marriage a chance?

7. Jack Magnus wrote in his Readers' Favorite Review "Cornelia Feye's Death of a Zen Master is a well-written and

absorbing story that harkens back to the classic murder mystery novels such as those penned by Agatha Christie." Did you recognize any similarities with Agatha Christie mysteries? How does this novel compare to other mystery writers you enjoy?

8. Do you meditate? What is your experience, if any, with meditation?

9. Did you have suspects for the murder mystery and were surprised by the resolution?

10. Did the description of the food at the Zen Retreat pique your appetite?

ACKNOWLEDGMENTS

To all the wise Zen teachers in my life, as well as the Dalai Lama, and above all the Buddha himself, I bow in gratitude. They guided me one a path to understanding instead of fill my head with knowledge and instructions.

Thich Nhat Hanh's commentaries on the Heart Sutra, as well as his other writings have been precious guideposts to deepening my meditation practice. The Deer Park Monastery founded by Thich Nhat Hanh has been a sanctuary for me and many others seeking refuge and peace for many years. It's untouched canyons, sweeping views, glorious meditation hall, and dharma talks by the founder as well as resident monastics are an inspiration.

The two Japanese Suzukis, Shunryu Suzuki and D.T. Suzuki, and their writings, particularly *Zen Mind, Beginner's Mind*, have provided inspiration and insight for me and thousands of others. They were the groundbreakers, who brought Zen philosophy to the western world. The Zen monasteries and retreats associated with the San Francisco Zen Center, founded by Shunryu Suzuki are centers of meditation, healing, and serenity and have inspired the settings of this novel – without any of the violent incidents, of course.

At the San Diego Zen Center, the Zen Masters Elizabeth Hamilton and Ezra Bayda have taught me tough lessons about humility and letting go of ego, and shared their wisdom.

∾

This novel would be a lot less consistent and readable without the valuable comments and feedback from my Sisters in Crime writing group members, Valerie Hansen, Suzanne Haworth, Kim Keeline, Nicole Larsen, and Suzanne Shephard.

My Beta readers Steven Bluhm, Mary Kay Gardner, and Elizabeth Siegler have provided additional feedback and constructive criticism, which improved the story and character development. I thank them for their time and interest.

Finally I thank my family, my husband Glen, and my sons Sebastian and Max for their ongoing support and love.

ABOUT THE AUTHOR

Cornelia Feye received her M.A. in Art History and Anthropology from the University of Tübingen, Germany. After five years in New York, she moved to San Diego, where she taught Eastern and Western Art History. Her museum experience includes the Mingei International, the San Diego Museum of Art, the Museum of Man, and the California Center for the Arts in Escondido. From 2007 to 2017 she was the School of the Arts and Arts Education Director at the Athenaeum, Music & Arts Library in La Jolla. Her first novel, *Spring of Tears*, an art mystery set in France won the San Diego Book Award for the mystery category in 2011. *House of the Fox*, a mystery set in Anza Borrego desert, and *Private Universe*, a coming-of-age story and art mystery, followed. She co-edited the short story anthology *Magic, Mystery & Murder*, with Tamara Merrill. It won the San Diego Book Award in 2019. The second short story anthology, *Modern Metamorphoses-Stories of Transformation*, was released in the summer of 2020. Publications include art historical essays and reviews in English and German. She is the founder of Konstellation Press, an independent publishing company specializing in genre fiction and poetry at the intersection of art, music and literature. www.konstellationpress.com

CPSIA information can be obtained
at www.ICGtesting.com
Printed in the USA
FSHW022107260820
73248FS